In Search of Grace

(2nd Edition)

Sister Lela

Your love and support mean the world to me!

Peace and Blessings,

Adrienne Smith

In Search of Grace

(2nd Edition)

Adrienne Smith

In Search of Grace
2018 by Adrienne Smith

All Rights Reserved Under
International and Pan-American Copyright Conventions.
No part of this book may be used or reproduced in any manner whatsoever
without written permission except in the case of brief quotations embodied
in critical articles or reviews.
Printed in the United States of America by GCG Publishing
Chesterfield, Missouri 63005

Dedication

This book is dedicated to my father, Wallace J. Edmondson II and my paternal grandmother, Gertrude Edmondson. Daddy, before you left this earth, you told me lots of stories about Grandma's past. You encouraged me to ask her to tell me more about her past. So, I did. And Grandma, you opened up to me about some things that have happened in your life. Not much about your two versions of the story matched, so I made it up! Thank you anyway. The things that you did say inspired my creativity. I'm so blessed to have had you in my life, Daddy; and to still have you in my life, Grandma. I will love you both forever!

I was blessed enough to have two fathers. Dad, you were as much a part of me as my own skin. You have always given me great advice. I miss that and you so very, very much. I dedicate this book to you too because you have also represented what a strong, real man should be.

Acknowledgments

I'd like to thank my Father in Heaven, my Lord and Savior, Jesus The Christ from whom all blessings flow. Thank you to Jill Mettendorf of GCG Printing and Si of Exsiting Creations for all of your professional help. I have to thank my sisters, Rhonda Smith, Siinya Edmondson, and Stacey Howes for listening to my ideas and supporting my work. Big thanks to thank their husbands, Barron Smith and Jesse Howes, for helping me to promote and market my book. Many thanks to my friend, LaKesha Dean, for your editing expertise as well. Shout out to my brother Edwin J. Kindall. And last, but certainly not least, I want to thank my son, Damion Smith. Son, you have supported me emotionally, financially, mentally, and so much more. From the bottom of my heart, Thank you.

This book is further dedicated to all of the smart, strong, brave women in my life and especially to the two who have passed on – my mother, Marcia Kindall and my maternal grandmother, Ada Ellis- for so many great stories. I love and miss you Mom and Nana!

All of you have shared some of your experiences with me that have blended together for a very hearty roux for my "grace" stew.

Thank you,
Adrienne "Angel" Smith

Foreword

To my sister (in-law) and my fellow author friend,

You said you were going to do it, and you did! I know it was a long time coming, but when the opportunity came for you to shut one window and open a new door, like the star you are, you rose to the occasion. I'm very proud of you and so happy for your readers.

If you are about to read this book, I assure you will love it. You will be on the edge of your seat, turning the next page to see what happens next. You will also cry a little, laugh a lot, and feel uplifted by the time you are done reading it. "Angel" is a wonderful story teller. And as she weaves together the lives of Karen, Mrs. Toni, Grace, and the other characters, you will be swept up in her words, her technique, and the poignant emotions that she is able to evoke in her readers. Be sure to recommend that everyone you know get a copy of the book. Buy one for yourself and gift a copy to someone else you know and love.

Peace,
Barron Smith,
Author of *From Getting Shot to Taking Shots*

Chapter 1

As I search for grace in my life, I must admit that all of my most profound moments begin with the woman who raised me.

As I search for grace in my life, I must admit that all of my most profound moments begin with the woman who raised me, which is why I cannot figure out how I got here. Again! It seems like it was just yesterday that I was packing my bags and going back to my grandmother's house. But today I thank God for her because that tired, no-good, so-called fiancé of mine is so undependable. I am such a fool.

"Hi Grandma."

"Hi Baby," at first sounding like her usual chipper self, but then, "What's wrong?" her voice suddenly becoming heavy laden with concern. *Silence.* "Karen, baby what's wrong?" now she was sound very worried.

Sniffles. I couldn't help it. I always cried when I felt like a fool.

"Karen Angelique Edmonds! You get your clothes and get the hell out of there! Now! Don't make me come get you! You know I will. And this time I'll bring BOTH my pistols!"

"I'm outside Grandma. Just open the door." I winced. My grandmother must also think that I am a fool too.

My grandmother was a feisty little thing. Just slightly over 4'6," she threw her little 115 pounds around freely. After my father died in a terrible car accident when I was only months old, my mother moved in with his mother. She had just had me. So, when Mama fell into a deep depression, Grandma, and even the doctors, thought it was just the Baby Blues. Eventually Mama stopped coming home at all and Grandma, and her best friend from next door, Mrs. Ethel, raised me. Mama was found dead in an abandoned apartment building from a crack overdose when I was just seven years old. When we speak of her life and her death we say, "Carolynn loved Kenny hard and mourned his death even harder. She died of a broken heart." We never speak of all the nights she didn't come home or of all the stories we heard around town about her doing all sorts of unmentionable things for a crack rock.

Grandma managed to work at night as a nurse to put me through college. I slept next door at Mrs. Ethel's house from kindergarten until about the time I turned sixteen. Mrs. Ethel was a widow whose husband worked for Union Pacific Railroad and invested in oil and gold. He left her with plenty of money but not one child. When I came home from school in the afternoons, Mrs. Ethel would be waiting for me on her front porch. We talked about my day while she fixed me a sandwich and a glass of milk. One day when it was peanut butter and honey day, I told her about Antoine.

"What's got you all smiling and carrying on today young lady?" she asked one day when I was in second grade.

"I don't know," I said smiling from ear-to-ear.

"Oh, I think you do know. You just don't want to tell me. That hurts, cause I thought we were friends; family even. Why, my grandmother and your grandmother Toni's grandmother were best friends. My mama and Toni's mama were best friends. Me and Toni two peas in a pod. I'm sure if me and Mr. Jeff had had a child, he would have been friends with your daddy. Now here you are not telling me what's got you so happy! I'm like your second grandmother, but that's okay," holding up one of her hands as if really stopping me. " I guess we are not as close as I thought."

"Oh yes we are Mrs. Ethel! You are my second grandmother. I got two grandmas, but if I tell you, you are going to tell my other grandma because you are best friends. And you can't tell her," I said.

"I won't tell."

The next day, Grandma walked me to school, which was unusual. She was usually too tired and feet hurt too badly to walk me the three blocks to my elementary school. She also stayed there half the day right by my side, which as even more unheard of. She kept asking me, "You got any *special* friends here?" So much for being my secret-keeping second grandmother.

After a quick snack after school each day, Mrs. Ethel would sit in front of the TV to watch her soap operas while I did homework. Then I would help her make dinner. I learned to cook by watching her snap peas, knead bread, and baste turkey. At night, we would watch game shows then I would take a bath and go to bed only to have my Grandma Toni wake me up with the sun on her back and coffee on her breath. "Good morning Love Bug," she'd sing. I don't know who cried harder when I finally left for college – Grandma or Mrs. Ethel.

Today, I came through the door and wanted to collapse into my grandmother's arms. I felt heavy and lonely. Defeated. But she was too busy putting fresh linens on my old bed and talking a mile a minute.

"I know he don't think you don't have a place to go. Umph! Even after I'm dead and gone to Glory, you will still have your own place to call home. This is YOUR house. You hear me?" she questioned but not really asking me.

She continued, " I learned the hard way thanks to The Old Woman that every woman needs her own. Own money. Own house. You have your own. Unlike his raggedy a– oops, forgive me Father – behind. Ain't got two wooden nickels to rub together. His mama don't either. Matter of fact, he is doing the best out of five living generations. Now that's sad." She continued. Grandma had finished tidying up the whole room by the end of her soliloquy.

Then, Grandma opened the curtains. She is standing and staring out of the window overlooking the backyard we spent so much time in. A little less irate, she says, "That's sad when your own children can't even come to you when they need help. I needed someone to help me. No one did. And it almost cost me my life. That boy NEEDS some help. But you can't help him. Oh no! You tried. Your degree is in Sociology, not psychology. That fool needs a head doctor."

My degree is in Anthropology and I minored in Jouralism; however, I was not going to correct her this time. I didn't have a chance to anyway because she kept fussing. "Ole dog! I knew he was no good. You too good for him. Uh huh, too good I tell you."

Actually, Antoine Blanks is good. He is a good man who makes bad choices. He was raised by a prostitute mother and a want-to-be pimp father. His father was too jealous to be a *real* pimp. All the insecurity drove him to an early grave. Right after he left his wife, Antoine's father died. The heart attack killed him before his body could even hit the ground. He always thought that his wife was cheating with one of her johns, but they found out after his death that he was actually the one cheating. He had six other children by four other women. Like my mother, Antoine's mother was deeply hurt by her husband's death and philandering. Left with five children of her own, she retreated into herself and closed the rest of the world out. Besides running the bed and breakfast out of her four-story historic home that she inherited from her parents and later lost in foreclosure, she did nothing else in life. Not even continue to raise Antoine, the youngest of her children. The streets raised him, which is how he got into the mess he is in now.

Mrs. Blanks rarely left the house except for weddings and funerals. It was like Antoine had no mother. My grandmother warned me about men who grew up like this. Yet, Antoine and I bonded over the losses in our lives. We took care of each other as children and as adults. In grade school, I shared my home-cooked lunches with him and he protected me from bullies. In high school, I cooked for him and he took good care of my car. In college, I helped him with his homework and he listened to my problems and was always there whenever I needed him. I also shared what my grandmother taught me about God. I poured into him and built him up in the areas where he had been so torn down. But he had some very dark secrets.

Chapter 2

Now I had seen enough Lifetime movies to know that something was not right.

Now, with my room as clean and neat as the day before I left home, I began to unpack. Grandma would have also unpacked for me; she was on a roll, but someone was at the door. I don't know why I packed all the lingerie Antoine bought me. I should have left it just like I left him. I sat there on my bed holding the cream-colored, completely see through, floor- length nighty with spaghetti straps and the side split all the way up to the hip. I thought about the day he purchased it for me. Our first big falling out. It was also the first time I saw my grandmother with her pistol in her hand. It was the one some man from her past bought it for her a long time ago. She said men always bought gifts for women when they messed up.

It was almost Valentine's Day when I got the lingerie and a life lesson from grandma. Antoine walked in and handed me the beautifully wrapped box from a Frontenac boutique. The packaging and ribbons were as elegant and pretty as what was usually in the box.

"Here Babe, Happy Love Day."

"It's not Valentine's Day yet honey," I said, even though I was excited about the gift.

He joked, "So you don't want it?" and pulled the box away.

"Not now. Keep it and give it to me when we come back from our Love Day dinner," I surrendered.   Antoine agreed,

"Okay, but we don't know what might happen on that day, so you might as well open it now.," he said. I thought that was a strange thing to say, but more importantly, I did not have a gift for him yet.

"Keep it until I come back from the mall, okay? Then we can exchange gifts," I added.

My soon-to-be husband was hard to shop for. He had superb taste and it *seemed* he spared no expense when it came to buying what he wanted for himself or for me. He worked hard and made good money, but did not really spend a lot of it for the designer clothes, shoes, coats, even underwear for us. He was a smart shopper and a professional haggler. I was always so nervous about buying things for him because I feared they would not be good enough. I had put off getting a Valentine's gift until two days before the big day for this reason. I had been successful in the past with all the different colognes I got for him. Scents was something I was good at. He loved every smell good item I bought him, unlike some of the suites, shirts, jeans, and caps I gifted him. We promptly returned those together so that he could pick out his own gift.

"I'll be back shortly Honey Bun, okay?" I called over my shoulder as I headed for the door. "Okay Babe" he barely got out before stuffing a homemade potato skin into his mouth and picking up the remote to the large flat screen plasma television he purchased after Thanksgiving last year from the well -known electronics store. Because he opened a line a credit with them, he got an additional 20 percent off the already 60 percent off 75 inch TV. Little did they know, the company would make no real money off of Antoine through finance charges because he paid it off in full, in cash the next week and closed out the account. He had been saving his income tax check from the beginning of the year especially for this occasion. The man was super smart with money.

I went to the Central West End to Cassey's, a custom fragrance shop, to make my own original scent for my baby. He was sure to love this. He liked anything that was different which is why he said he liked me. I wasn't like all the other girls. However, cologne inventing and purchasing took a lot longer than I thought. First, I was given a mini- lesson on fruit and citrus scents, woodsy and musk scents, clean and airy scents, and so on. I finally bought a clean but masculine scent.

Then I took flowers to my mother's grave; something I did every holiday and her birthday. By the time I got home it was dark; the house was even darker. And strangely quiet. I put down all of the gifts. I bought him gourmet chocolate turtle truffles too because he is also a candy-holic. That's another reason why he liked me – he said I was so sweet.

"Tony!" I rarely called him that because it is my grandmother's name. Besides, I didn't like the idea of calling him what all his boys called him. When the name slipped from my lips however, I got a creepy feeling across my skin. I should have known that all of hell was about to break loose. My grandmother always says a woman should always trust her gut. "God gave us that gift so that we can detect men's mess," she would say.

"Antoine!" I shouted a bit louder more for myself than for him because I was unnerved. "Sweetie, where are you?" I went from room to room in our spacious apartment that neither of us could afford alone. Of course the furniture was all exquisite as well. We both had good taste in furnishings and decor.

He was not in the dining room, kitchen, den, home office, bathroom, or bedroom. Finally, I went to the door of the spare bedroom, which was closed. Because it usually stays open, I twisted the knob and proceeded to walk through it all at the same time only to run face first into its non-moving structure. The door was locked from the inside. I smiled and knocked thinking that this wonderful man was going to have a wonderful surprise for me in there. From the sounds beyond the door, the bump from my face and then my knock startled him, and he was uttering "huh?" and "what?" and "who is it?" and vigorously moving about. Now I had seen enough Lifetime movies to know that something was not right. I screamed, "What the hell are you doing in there? Open the damn door!"

Now, I do not know what my father was like. I heard he was a kind and gentle soul with a free spirit. My grandma, his mother, Toni, was quite the opposite extreme. She was never very gentle with anything or anyone except me. So, I guess I must have channeled my inner-Toni. Like she would have, I began to beat on the door and yell profanely. "You better not have a bitch in there. So, help me God, I will blow both your heads off!" I did not own a gun, but I knew someone who did.

My grandmother always talked about the firearms men gave her, including my grandfather. He was a police officer and said she was just the right size for someone to want to do something to her but not big enough to stop them. My grandfather insisted that she learn how to shoot and legally own her own weapon. I never saw them, but I knew of them. I also knew that my grandmother's past left her with a great need to protect herself.

I pulled out my cell phone and called my grandmother screaming and crying and insisting that the love of my life had another woman in our home locked up in the spare bedroom. She was furious. I forgot to tell her to bring her pistol, so when she said "We are on our way," I assumed she meant she and Mrs. Ethel would come. Instead, she and Smith and Wesson were there in 27 minutes. I don't know how she made the 40- minute trip so quickly. And my other grandmother was nowhere in sight.

I was sitting in front of the guest bedroom door on the floor rocking and crying. Antoine was on the other side of the door. I could hear that he was crying too. Oddly enough, I did not hear the woman. Because I did not have a free hand to lock the front door when I first came in, my grandmother was able to walk right into the apartment and was standing over me waving her gun wildly recommending that Antoine and his "hoe" come out right now or she would shoot the lock off. Nothing.

"Ima count to two," grandma began. Huh? Who counts to just two? Evidently, she did not have time for anything past two. "And if your ass ain't out here, my ass is coming in there to get you and Jezebel. One!" Toni Rene Edmonds shot the door handle and all that was left was a huge gaping hole in the middle of the door.

I covered my ears and jumped back, for now I was standing behind her unable to believe my grandmother was acting like a shrunken John Wayne. I pushed the door open thinking I was going to find my fiancé and/or his concubine shot to death. Instead, I saw what was first unrecognizable, but then somehow very familiar simultaneously.

Chapter 3

I didn't allow you to stay with your mama, and I am not letting you stay with this…

The first time that my grandmother used a firearm she was eleven years old. The Old Woman, that is what she called her father's mistress who helped to kidnap and raise her, had hit her so hard across the face that she spun around in a complete circle once. "Didn't I tell you not to go outside? Are you deaf *and* dumb?" The old woman may have said some other mean and hurtful things too, but grandma was focused on the gun on the table behind the old woman. She heard nothing else,

Little Toni said, "Yeah, you did. I'm sorry." Then she slowly walked past the old woman toward the table where she usually sat to read and do homework where the gun was. The old woman thought that she had won the round. Smugly, she gave a grunt and walked away without looking back. That is until the shot rang out and whizzed dangerously close past her head. The bullet lodged itself into the door frame ahead of her.

That was the last time the old woman had hit Toni Renee Edmonds. Today, however, she was a marksman.

"What the hell!?" I screamed, yet it felt like the high-pitched question that was really more like a statement came from somebody else. "Baby get out, get out. Mrs. Toni get out of here. Get her out of here!" Antoine was yelling. The love of my life was lying naked on the queen size bed on top of the covers and using a pillow to cover his man parts. A pornographic movie was mutely playing on the TV and on the floor next to the bed was a jar of Vaseline, a cigarette lighter, and a burned and blackened crack pipe. He was alone; no woman was in the room.

The room was smoky and smelled of molding bread and dirty gym socks – a weird combination, especially for this room because it was never used. My grandmother stepped around me and calmly said, "I'll get her out of here alright. Come on Ms. Karen Edmonds, you will not become Mrs. Antoine 'Crackhead' Blanks on my watch."

My grandmother turned to walk out but tried to take my arm with her. "Wait. I don't understand," I said confused. I pulled away and ran back into the room. Antoine had laid back on the bed flat on his back. He had both hands over his face. The once captive pillow lay still defenseless and covering his family jewels. His eyes were somehow both big and small at the same time. His skin was gray. He was clammy, and his breath smelled awful. I grabbed his hand and snatched it away from his face. "Antoine, what's going on?" I asked confused. I had never known him to used drugs before.

"Come on Karen, we have to go. No granddaughter of mine will be staying with no crack-head. I didn't allow you to stay with your mama, and I am not letting you stay with this..." grandma was saying while, I began to look under the bed and in the walk-in closet. I looked behind the curtains and in the guest bathroom. There was no one else there. I *needed* there to be another woman in there. I could handle that. Grandma and I could have shot up the place and sent Antoine and his concubine running out of here. But this...this was different. I wasn't prepared for this. I also was not prepared for my grandmother to walk up behind me, pick me up, and carry me out the front door either. Bam-bam has nothing on Toni Edmonds.

Chapter 4

I'll call the police and tell them I'm about to choke the hell out of each one of you if you ever treat this child like this again.

I had not been in my old bedroom since my last year of college. Back then I had come home for Christmas and told my two grandmothers that I was getting married. Neither of them looked pleased. "Y'all remember Antoine, don't you?" Mrs. Ethel let a very dry "uh huh" ooze from her lips. Grandma said nothing. "Well, he asked me to marry him. I said yes," I said excitedly. The room was so quiet I questioned whether I had actually said anything. They were both sitting there as if I had not just given them the best news of my life. And then to make matters worse, they started talking to each other *about* me as if I was not there.

"Well, at least she is finishing school," one grandmother said. "I don't know. She still has one more semester. Maybe she too in love to go back in January," said the other grandmother. "Naw, that fool wants her to graduate and get a good job so that she can buy him some more pretty clothes and a fancy car. He ain't got no education. Didn't have sense enough to finish, so he probably wants her to graduate so she can get a good job and take care of him. You see she ain't got no ring from him," one of them was saying, but I couldn't tell which one because they were starting to blend into one big hateful hot mess. Besides, what were they talking about?

Antoine almost finished college himself. He ran track and got a scholarship to an HBCU. The first and only person in his family to go to college. He only came home to take care of his mother. She got sick and didn't have anyone to run her home that she had turned into a bed and breakfast. All of her other children turned their backs on her for some reason. Even one of Mr. Blanks' *other* sons as Mrs. Ethel called him, who lived with her for a while because his mother threw him out was now nowhere around. Actually, he had served time in jail for attempted murder.

Located right by the interstate, The Blanks Bed and Breakfast's business boomed with truckers and vacationers setting out to see the great United States one state at a time, especially in the summer. When it was Missouri's turn, everyone had to come taste Mrs. Blanks delicious cooking. That woman could burn the flame off of fire. She was also still known for turning a trick or two. Antoine had to go home and run the business when she got sick. Unfortunately, he never returned back to school.

He and his mother made good money. The Lord only knows what Mrs. Blanks spent her money on because she never had any. She constantly "borrowed" money from her son. Of course, she rarely ever paid it back. But Antoine bought nice clothes and shoes for himself. He even had a very nice luxury car. He said he would get me a ring when he could save and find a good deal on the perfect one. No starter ring for his fiancé.

Memories. That's all they are now that I finally left Antoine. While hanging up my work clothes in the tiny closet now however; and putting my other things in the massive chest of drawers, I listened to the voices downstairs. It was my other grandmother- number two- at the door. I called her the Quiet Storm. Where Grandma Toni was quick-tempered, loud, and would cuss in a heartbeat and ask The Lord for forgiveness, unless she was violently mad, Grandma Ethel was slow to anger, but once she was, look out!

I remember one time I got into a fight at school with a girl who chanted that my mama *and* daddy were junkies and that my grandmothers were lesbian lovers. We argued. She swung. I swung. I'm not sure what all happened next, but when I came to, she had to get stitches over her right eye and had a slight concussion. My principal wanted to suspend me for the rest of the school year and then have me transferred to the alternative school where all the "lil monsters," as my grandmothers called them, went. It almost happened too because my grandmother was already at work. And she had to work a double shift. I had no one to advocate for me. I called Quiet Storm.

Mrs. Ethel was not my legal guardian and was told by my principal to stay out of it. She was already upset about having to turn her black-eyed peas off to drive to my school when they called her, now that she was there, she was told to stay out of it. She refused to see me be "carted off to some animal house for bad kids because some heifer got what she deserved." Her words, not mine.

She called the police on herself after she told the principal, my teacher, whom I adored; the secretary, and the security officer where they could go and what they could do to themselves once they got there. This was the first time I had ever seen *this* grandmother go nuts. She barked out instructions and had everyone running around the principal's office like wild geese.

"Ms. Larson, sit your lil skinny ass back down in that lil chair behind that desk before I really give you something to gawk at. Mr. man or whatever your name is, I suggest you try to SECURE yourself a safe spot over there in that corner before I break your GOOD arm. Ms. Wallace and Dr. Flagg, you apologize to my child and let her know how wrong you were for treating her like a criminal and calling her grandmother away from preparing a hot, home cooked meal for her dinner this evening. Go on, open your mouths" Grandma Ethel said.

They stood and looked quite bewildered at Mrs. Ethel. "NOW! I'll call the police and tell them I'm about to choke the hell out of each one of you if you ever treat this child like this again. Everyone has the right to defend herself, even children" she demanded. They all started talking at the same time. They even shook my hand one by one apologizing.

My Grandma Ethel and I walked out of my school after she cradled the receiver back onto the telephone and sat outside on the steps of the school. "Lord, child," she began back to her normal self, "you about to see Mrs. Ethel go to jail. This is not even what I planned to do with you today." The police never came.

She was downstairs now. Hurricane Ethel was furious. I guess she had already been filled in by Grandmother number one, although I have no idea when she could have called her with the revelation that my Antoine was a drug addict. "All those fancy clothes were just a cover up for his ugly behavior. I knew it! I know all too well when a man is hiding something. Don't no man laugh and smile as much as his big grown self does. Ole clown!" she said almost in one breath as if they were in the middle of a conversation instead of at the beginning of one as I thought they were.

Grandma Toni gently closed the door behind Mrs. Ethel and said, "I can't let my baby go through that. She is too good. I didn't let her own mama drag her through the mud. I'm definitely not about to let the son of a whore and a dog-in-heat do it. No sir, over my dead body." She was surprisingly very calm when she said it and she did not use any profanity. Of course, she was not calling on God either. This was very strange seeing their roles reverse. I love them both; don't know what I would ever do without them, but they never cease to amaze – or should I say confuse me. I went downstairs.

"Are you alright?" they both asked almost at the same time when I walked into the living room. They looked so strained and old. Grandma Toni's shoulders slumped forward as if she had just lost her best friend. I felt the way that she looked. I was also very confused. Why did Grandma keep saying she did not "let" my mother hurt me with her drug use? Didn't Mama leave me? I thought we learned of her drug use when we learned of her death. The rumors started AFTER her death.

I was also very concerned about Antoine. When did he begin using drugs? Why was he using drugs? Was there ever a good reason? I wanted to get back home and find out. Intelligent, God-fearing men did not smoke crack rocks. I knew the granny duo wouldn't let me leave right now. So, I decided to call him instead.

"I'm fine. I need to make some phone calls though," I told them. "Take your time Love Bug, I'll make you something to eat," My grandmother said as she tried to get up from her chair.

I did not want any dinner; I wanted my life to go back to normal, but I also wanted to keep my grandmother occupied while I called home. "Okay, Grandma." Then Mrs. Ethel added, "And I'm going to run back next door and get this banana nut bread I made this morning. We can have that for dessert. May help us figure out how to kill that sucker and get rid of the body before his coo- coo for cocoa puffs mama even realize he is missing."

With that, she draggled, not ran as she claimed she would and usually could, to her house next door. It pained me to see her like that. She had aged right before my eyes. The realization coated me with thoughts of my needing to protect and take care of them now. I'm not a little girl anymore who could run off to my two grandmothers who were anything but gay. Men chased them and they let them. They were the life of the Bingo party. No, I was not going to ever tell them about any problems in my life ever again. I have to take care of myself.

Chapter 5

I learned to associate the dark with doom.

Back then, I walked in on Antoine many more times locked in one of the rooms of our home jacking off, watching porn, and smoking crack. More times than I can even admit to myself because that would require admitting how many times I left him then came back. He tried to get slicker with using. That only made me get wiser about it. He agreed to counseling. It did not help because he never wanted to be honest about his drug use. He talked about how his father treated his mother. How withdrawn his mother is. How he hardly ever sees or talks to his sisters and brothers, not even Ren who lived with him and his mother for five years when his mother, one of his father's mistresses, put him out. Ren and Antoine became very close. I later found out just how close.

He went through several counselors to deal with this and other problems. I would always get fed up with him not being as forthcoming as possible about drugs. I would bring up what I thought was his real problem. Each of the counselors agreed that these were all serious issues that could manifest themselves in many self-destructive ways if not handled. They already had. But they agreed that the substance abuse needed to be handled immediately.

I soon grew tired of going through the motions of therapy. I knew it could never help because of the secrets Antoine was trying to keep. Grandma noticed the stench of defeat on me and told me something that changed my life.

Grandma had always told me that she was not sure of her exact age nor of where she was born. I knew that this was common for people born in the south a long time ago. Grandma never went into details until the day I slumped into her kitchen chair almost knocking over the entire table. She didn't ask what was wrong. She did not make any of her "if it walks like a dog and it barks like a dog, it's probably Antoine" jokes. She just started unwinding her tale.

> *I remember playing around the big tree in our front yard with my little sister. My mama and papa had five children. Agatha and I were the youngest two. We always played outside while mama fixed dinner. We played until my daddy came home from work. Daddy was always dirty and sweaty, but he would swoop Agatha and me up in his big ole arms and carry us inside to eat. We would giggle because even though Daddy smelled like soot and was covered from head to toe with something as*

black as the ace of spades, we loved him.

But on this day, Daddy didn't come walking up to the house. He drove up in a car that I had never seen before. And he was clean, shaven, and dressed in nice clothes. A woman got out and came over to Agatha and me. She said, 'Come on babies. Your daddy is going to take you for a ride in his new car.' We looked toward Daddy and he beckoned us with his massive hand. We took off running for the car. Once we saw our poppa, we knew it was alright. We trusted him.

Once my sister and I were tossed into that car, Daddy took off lighting fast. The woman barely got the door closed behind her before he shot off. We drove for a long while. When the car finally stopped, I knew something was not right. I cried for my mama but the woman fussed, "Shut up." Daddy parked the car behind an old barn and we all got out. He left the car there and we all started walking. It was getting darker and darker outside. I learned to associate the dark with doom.

Eventually, we saw a motionless train up ahead. Daddy said, "Hurry on now. We have to jump it before time to pull out." He switched Agatha to his other arm and picked me up in his free arm. He ran toward the train and the woman was on his heels. Agatha began to cry. She was hungry. We both were. And we wanted to go home to our mama.

We jumped on that train and it eventually pulled away from what would soon be our past. Agatha and I never saw our mama again. And The Old Woman never let us forget that she was not our mama, especially once Daddy left her.

You see Love Bug, my daddy had been having an affair with that old bi-

*I mean woman. They stole Agatha and me from our mama; from
our home. My daddy left my mama alone with three other kids.
Never saw them again either. It wasn't long before he left The Old Woman too.*

*Can you believe he left me with that awful woman? Me. His child. His flesh and
blood. And Aggie too. He left the both of us. He didn't say goodbye. We had no
idea that he wasn't coming back until he didn't come back any more. I trusted
him Karen. He was my father. He owed a responsibility to me. He let me down
in a big way. And for what? Because he could. People will let you down, Bug.
That is the only thing you can count on in this life.*

Chapter 6

Deep inside I knew this would all be someone's demise. I just prayed not mine.

I also left home a few more times after first learning about Antoine's habit. I never went back to Grandma's house until now, however. I never even told either of the warrior women who protected me and whom I called Grandma, about it, although I think they suspected. I left because drugs and porn were taking over his life as well. He had even started sneaking out of the house at odd hours of the morning while I was asleep in order to go to the strip club. When I confronted him about it, he said he was not *sneaking* and that I was making a big deal out of nothing; all men do it.

He continued, "First of all, I'm a grown ass man and can do whatever the hell I want to do and can go wherever the hell I want to go. It's my money. You are not wanting for anything. All the bills are paid, and I still come home to you. Secondly, it's nothing. All men get a little extra eye candy one way or another. Would you rather I look at your friends and other women while I'm with you? That's what my boys do."

I knew this was madness that was only going to get worse. When we talked about his drug use, he said Ren, his half-brother, turned him on to marijuana and porn when he was ten. When he was in high school, he started lacing his joints with cocaine like all the other boys did that he and Ren hung out with in the neighborhood. He was still friends with many of these thugs, another sore spot in our lives. Now he was smoking crack ang frequenting the bootie bars. I saw this as a steady downward spiral. I feared he would die soon. He insisted that he had control over it.

He argued, "When I went away to college, I didn't smoke or use anything. That was three straight years Karen. And everybody down south was smoking, snorting, or shooting something in those days. I stayed away from it all, Babe. That proves I can control it – it doesn't control me. Now I just do it when I get stressed. It's no big deal," he tried to say with conviction.

His addiction to porn really began when he was seven years old, before his brother shared movies and weed with him. When he was seven years old, he heard his mother and father arguing one evening. "Which one of your whores is it this time Vernon, huh?" he would hear his mother say. After a long and heated verbal brawl, the springs in his parent's bed began to bounce. Besides his mother's screams of ecstasy, Antoine would always hear another woman's wails and screams of "It's yours, Daddy! All yours!" seemingly from the television. His father would let out a few hard, loud grunts as well as if he was being descended upon by a giant man-eating vulture with a few "Oh God" in there before he let out one really long, really loud moan of ecstasy and then a final "Damn!" But it also always seemed to Antoine that while his father was creating a symphony of sex, another man was insisting on an answer to, "Is this my pussy? Who's is it, huh?!" It was a long time later before Antoine discovered that it was a pornographic movie helping his parents make all the noise in their bedroom.

After a night of rough sex by porn-light, they would both fall asleep immediately after for some hours then Mr. Blanks would get up, freshen up, and leave. The next morning Antoine would find his mother cooking breakfast for the truckers who were occupying the downstairs rooms for rent with a big smile on her face. Her happiness never lasted long. The cycle of getting caught, fighting about it, having sex while watching dirty movies, and then his father leaving his mother on her own personal high only to crash by the next day continued until his father died.

Even though his mother's happiness was always short lived, he still wondered what made her so vocal and happy when his father was in her bedroom. He knew they were watching something on television, so he went to their bedroom to explore for answers. When he learned of his parent's secret pleasure, one of the video tapes became his favorite past-time behind his locked door while his mother was busy in the house and his father was God only knows where. He encouraged his friends to watch porn too. Watching porn turned from an adolescent pastime to a full blown grown-man addiction. By the time he asked for my hand in marriage and I discovered his addiction, he had over two thousand pornographic DVDs. I knew like his drug use, that this monster would soon spin more out of control as well. I expressed my concern to Antoine.

"Today it's watching ass on TV, tomorrow it will be watching live ass in strip clubs, and next week it will be humping every Tina, Dorothy, and Henrietta in town!" I warned this man way back then. Turns out, it was more than a warning. It was a premonition. Whatever you do not want to exist, do not ever speak it into the universe as though it is so.

He proposed again just to shut me up, this time with a beautiful ring with a stone as big as my head. It worked. Kind of. Deep inside I knew this would all be someone's demise. I just prayed not mine. We found a wonderful church home where the Pastor and the other members were loving and supportive. They also had a phenomenal Marriage Ministry for their members and people in the community who were married or had a date set to be married. We learned a lot and even went on a retreat.

All of the couples took turns researching and then presenting information on a different relationship topic each month. By the time it was our turn to cover "Supporting One Another Even Through Tough Times," I began to feel like we were making progress. All of the couples raved about how well we did. They said we seemed relaxed and knowledgeable. Some even said we seemed so in sync with one another and knew we would have a successful marriage. I was beginning to feel that way too. I thought Antoine did as well. He was not using drugs during this time and said that he had given his porn collection to his friend Troy. I wanted him to take the large trash bags of movies down to the river and watch them sink to the bottom, but Troy was the devil in the flesh. I figured his soul could not be damaged any further.

Even that addictive relationship seemed to be dissipating as we met and became friends with other couples in the church, including the Pastor and First Lady, who were the same age as we were. I truly believed that we were on the right path, and with the wedding just eleven months away and my 3.5 carat diamond ring on my finger, why wouldn't I? I had not learned yet that my soon to be husband was really a Master of Disguise.

Chapter 7

It didn't make sense to me that love and destruction could both be present in the same heart.

I had resorted to going to other people's homes when Antoine and I fell out; however, I couldn't go to Mrs. Blanks' house again, nor did I want to go to the homes of my friend from church, or my co-workers' homes, or a hotel any more. It was too cumbersome to drag my clothes and shoes around. I always left something I needed at home. Other people's houses were not clean, they smoked too much, their beds were too lumpy or springy if they had a bed for me at all. I slept on the floor at my future mother-in-law's tiny apartment, and I missed the hell out of my man. Besides, I was really embarrassed to show up on someone's doorstep with my bag in my hand and tears in my eyes. Everyone always knew the source of my predicament much to my chagrin.

I even checked into a hotel room a few times. That was getting very expensive, however. Antoine was not getting any over-time at work anymore. He said most of the workers were new and they were not filling as many orders for large refrigeration parts at the plant, Hussmann's, as they used to – no incentive pay. I was paying a lot more of the bills by myself. I found myself regretting that we took such an expensive apartment. I loved the place. Antoine loved it too. He said he was never going to let me leave him because he needed me to help with the bills for his Never Land. I would feign hurt and he would laugh and put his arms around me saying, "Baby Cakes, you know I'm just playing. I love you more than the moon and the stars." Now that money was so tight, his playful days filled with laughter were few and far in-between.

I didn't understand how so much good could exist in the same man who also was full of so much darkness. I didn't get how one man could be so warm then turn around and be so frigid. It didn't make sense to me that love and destruction could both be present in the same heart. It was clear that Antoine was two people. One of his selves was charming and funny. Handsome and full of valor. Gentle and protective. His other self was common and grimy. Distant and hurtful. Reckless and ugly. He treated himself like he hated him. Besides having to lie to me to cover his self-hatred, he treated me very well. Or at least I thought he did. Out of nowhere, he would begin to act strange. He would not talk to me very much. When he did, he did not make eye contact with me. When he did kiss me, it was only on the lips, not deep passionate French kisses as he usually did. He didn't touch me; he always had an excuse to not make love. He even sat in his car once parked in front of our house while talking on the phone. Not for a few minutes but 30 to 35 minutes, sometimes an hour.

He seemed to be in a bad mood all the time, but never wanted to talk about it. Of course, I started looking for signs of his using drugs again. He had either become a pro at hiding it or it was something else besides drugs. Another woman?

I checked our bank accounts twice each day. I even checked his personal account for missing money. I reviewed his pay check stubs and receipts for purchases. I looked at his eyes, lips, and legs which usually told on him when he used. His lips would turn very dark, almost black. But they were fine. His eyes would seem glassed over. But they were fine as well. He also lost weight instantly when he had been smoking crack even after just one weekend. The weight loss would start in his legs which were big and strong like the rest of him. After smoking a few rocks, his legs would begin to resemble twigs. But he had not lost any weight and looked healthy.

His fingertips were not hard and dark like they are when he would smoke primos, marijuana joints laced with cocaine, either. His breath did not smell bad. I even checked it in his sleep. I followed him unbeknownst to him only to discover that he sometimes went to his mother's house, their old neighborhood, or the cemetery where his father was buried. All real nice son-like gestures, but all the other behaviors were so unlike him.

I tried to talk to him about it. He would always say, "It's nothing." I tried to use some of the tools we learned in Marriage Ministry. "Honey, I need you to be a giver of grace right now. Talk to me even though you don't want to or feel like you can." He insisted it was nothing and would walk away irritated.

"Come on Pooh," using the pet name I gave him in middle school, "Pastor said once per month each of us gets to pull the Grace Card. You have to do something that I am asking you to do even though you really don't want to. I want you to talk to me about whatever is going on. Come on," I sweetly asked.

"I'm unhappy. Okay, there. I said it. I don't know why," he admitted. I was shocked when my true love said this to me. I was speechless…for a few seconds. Then, I wasn't sweet anymore. I was angry.

"Unhappy?! Unhappy?! What the hell do you have to be so unhappy about?!" I asked. His attempt at walking way succeeding this time. He walked right out the door. I wished he would have driven his unhappy self into the river. He was acting bipolar. I would talk to him about seeing a physician this time. Someone who could check him out physically instead of just a head doctor. My grandma was right, I could not help him with this.

After a full evaluation and a physical, I learned that Antoine had been diagnosed with depression as a teen. This dark condition had reared its ugly head again. Why didn't he tell me he spent many hours as a teenager on the couch in a family therapist office? He was placed on medicine but took himself off of it when he went away to college. All of this was news to me. Who was he? I felt like I didn't know him at all. How many other secrets was he keeping from me?

Chapter 8

Write a book that people really want to read and you will soar with the eagles!

We postponed the wedding. We needed to give his system time for the new medicine to work. Antoine needed to get back to happy as Terry McMillan would say. I stayed right by his side. I have lots of good qualities, but my best one is my sense of loyalty. Antoine admitted that he was glad that I did not leave him. Not just because of the apartment, but seriously. He said he needed me.

Grandma and her partner in crime were pleased as punch that the wedding was on hold. "It will only be a matter of time before he messes up so badly that even YOU can't forgive him," Grandma said. I had developed quite an intimate relationship with God and prayed that I would always be able to forgive and love.

"Okay Grandma, so we are not getting married in August. But by Christmas, I will be Mrs. Blanks though. You wait and see" I told them. Mrs. Ethel looked at her and said, "Don't hold your breath," before they both laughed hysterically. What kind of grandmother feels this way about her only grandchild's upcoming nuptials? And I had two of them! Lord, give me strength.

Mrs. Ethel keeps telling me, "Baby, your grandmother really does understand how you feel. She loved a no-good man before and has a story too." I gave her some kind of look because I had always heard that my grandfather was an earthly angel. It's where my father got it from. Mrs. Ethel said, "Don't look at me like that. You need to have her tell you about her past, which consisted of more than just Eddie, your grandfather. She is ashamed about it, but it's true. I know, I was there. Ask her about it."

"Why Mrs. Ethel? If she is ashamed about it, let's just let it go," I said. The thought of making my grandmother even the slightest bit uncomfortable did not sit well with me at all. I love her dearly and would fight a bear in the woods over a honey pot with one hand tied behind my back for her. There was no way I was going to ask her about her past. The very same past she refused to say anything to me about.

I have overheard her talking about her father and the "Old Woman" with Mrs. Ethel when they both thought I was sleep. It didn't sound nice. My grandmother sounded so hurt and sad. Her father hurt her and the woman who raised my grandmother sounded like a monster. I never wanted anything to hurt her again. Not even her memories.

Mrs. Ethel answered, "You always writing those boring articles for those journals on dead things and old bones like that's really going to tell you something about people today. It really is not going to tell you anything about people. You need to write your grandmother's memoirs. We will all be rich!"

"Mrs. Ethel, you already have money, what are you talking about?" I questioned.

She said, "I'm talking about leaving this lil change to you and you will be broke in a year's time after you buy one of them fancy houses and foreign cars. Then you will be pecking with the chickens. Write a book that people really want to read and you will soar with the eagles!"

Grandma says in Mrs. Ethel's story, no one killed or got killed, stole, raped, or kidnapped, but she swears it is quite interesting and book worthy too. Why are old folks always so secretive about their pasts?

Chapter 9

I know that when the chips are down, my boys have always been there for me.

The seasons passed, and Antoine began to act like his old self. We realize now that money stress is a trigger for Antoine that made him want to resort back to the old habits he picked up from his half- brother when they were children. He was feigning for a hit. Fighting against the desire was putting him in a foul mood.

I was so happy to see him feeling better. He was having weekly counseling sessions with our Pastor. He took himself off of the medication again, but our Pastor agreed saying, "The Lord was the best mind regulator." I was a little worried about this but was eager to talk about planning our wedding and our future.

"Sweetie, do you want to get married before all the hustle and bustle of Christmas or wait until after Christmas to jump the broom?" I asked. Antoine said he wanted to marry me right then and there. I love this man so much. So many of my friends complain about their men running away from the very mention of marriage. Antoine wanted a normal life so badly. He didn't have one growing up. He had to raise himself and his mom after she became a recluse. He also wanted to be in right standing with God. A righteous man. A Joshua Man.

He explained, "I want to do this right and stop shacking up. It's time for you to be my wife. Besides, I think Mrs. Toni and Mrs. Ethel think I'm going to try to wiggle out of it. I can show them better than I can tell them," he said and then kissed me so deeply I thought I would faint.

Antoine asked why we couldn't get married on Christmas day. "No way!" I said in total shock, "No one would come to our ceremony. People want to spend the holidays with their families," I exclaimed. What he said next melted my heart. "All that matters to me is you, my mama, and your two grandmamas are there. I don't need anyone else around."

We each found two places that we want to use for the reception and together looked at all four venues. We settled on one that I loved the most and put down a down payment. My two grandmothers agreed to pay off the balance. Antoine couldn't believe they were willing to help. I knew they would come around.

"Thank you, Grandma. Thank you, Mrs. Ethel. I'm glad you two are finally on board," I said.

They exchanged glances with one another the way I had grown accustomed to seeing them do over the years and Mrs. Ethel said, "Girl, ain't nobody on board with this fiasco. But since you insist on marrying this boy, we decided to make a bet on how long it will last. The loser has to give the winner back her money," and they fell out laughing. I was hurt. Enough is enough. "You two are supposed to be saved, spirit-filled women of God. You should be ashamed of yourselves treating people like this, especially family!" I thought I had gotten to them because they were quiet and lowered their heads like two little girls who had been reprimanded for being bad...until I walked away and heard them burst into loud giddy laughter again. Maybe Antoine and I should just elope.

We settled on a spring wedding date in late April. Grandma and I shopped for my wedding gown. She and Mrs. Ethel interviewed and sampled catering companies. Antoine looked for a small orchestra for the church, a DJ for the reception, and a limousine to whisk us off to the hotel. We would take a honeymoon in a few years because there was not enough time to plan it nor pay for it. Together we made a guest list.

When it came time to addressing the invitations and mail them off, Antoine did not know the real or full names of his closest friends. "What did you think when we were making the list and I had you write down Tre, Bug, El, Boogie, and Chick?" he asked me smirking. I thought he was joking of course. He was going to have to hand deliver those.

I questioned, "How can you consider these guys your closest friends when you don't even know their names?" He got quiet. Pensive. He said, "I know that when the chips are down, my boys have always been there for me. I know that no matter what, they don't judge me; they accept me for who I am. I know that they have and always will lay down their lives for me. In my mind, their last names are Blanks because we are brothers." Yeah right; we will see.

Everything was all settled, and the wedding was a month away. I was so excited, I could hardly sleep. One night I got up to tiptoe into the kitchen for an apple and then into the living room to watch television until I felt sleepy again. I noticed Antoine was already out of bed. When I saw that he was not in the kitchen or the living room, I became suspicious. My heart skipped a beat. My stomach became queasy and I thought I would poop on myself. Where was he?

I screamed, "ANTOINE JAMAR BLANKS! WHERE THE HELL ARE YOU?" The bathroom door swung open and he rushed out with his pajama bottoms around his ankles and a *Mens's Health* magazine in his hand. "Babe, what's wrong? What's the matter?" he asked.

I was so relieved to see that he had only been sitting on the toilet and not locked in a room getting high that I ran and jumped into his arms and cried in his neck. He understood. I was forever scarred.

Chapter 10

Why are you interviewing the hottie?

My co-workers gave me a bridal shower. We took a two-and-a-half-hour lunch where we dined on grilled salmon, garlic shrimp, and lobster bisque; and drank mimosas at Dennigan's in Clayton. They showered me with a lot of gifts and advice.

It was my boss' idea to videotape the ladies giving me their best marriage/relationship advice. One lady, Mrs. Emma-Jean, who has been married for 32 years said, "Don't start anything that you cannot continue doing for the rest of your lives. Men are like puppies in more ways than one – if you feed them, you will always have to feed them. If you scratch their bellies, you will always have to do that. If you forgive their indiscretions, well you know the rest," she chided. We all laughed. I laughed hard on the outside but thought even harder on the inside. Could I ever forgive Antoine for cheating on me?

"Forgive your husband and everyone else for that matter, including yourself, seventy times seven hundred times like the Lord told us to do," another woman from Editing said. She was always misquoting the bible. Then she continued, "Forgive like He forgives us. Now, I'm not saying that it will always be easy, but it will always be the right thing to do,". She was divorced twice, and her last ex-husband was always trying to get her to come back to him. I wonder what the story was there.

"Okay, okay, okay, it's my turn," my boss, Sheila said. We were the same age. She has been with her boyfriend for eight years. She wanted to get married but did not want to run him off. She said Damon was a very good man. The best she ever met. He never brought up matrimony, however, and would always talk circles around the subject when other people asked them about a date.

"I know I am not an expert, but I do know a little something, my boss and good friend began"

"Shut up Sheila!" one of the girls yelled. "You're right, you are not an expert. If you were you would have a ring on it by now," followed another. The small private room erupted with laughter from all the women. I think we were a bit tipsy.

Sheila continued, "Karen, whoever and whatever that man is, is who and what he will always be. If there is something about him that you do not want in your life, do not marry him." The room fell silent. "If you marry him knowing things about him that are not right, it is up to you to find a way to live with it," she ended. Damn! She really had me thinking. I traded my orange juice only glass for one mixed with Champagne. I needed a real drink.

The girls and I had a wonderful time at the restaurant. On the following weekend, my friend from church, Bria, gave me a bachelorette party on the same night that Antoine had his bachelor party. My nerves were on edge and I felt sick to my stomach. The wedding was exactly one week away. Next Saturday, I would be Mrs. Blanks. Maybe that's why I felt queasy.

"Come on girl, get with it. I hired four fine male dancers for your party. You better get yourself together," Bria said.

"B, I just want to say, 'I do.' I don't know what possessed you to go all out with this stripper madness. That's not even my thing. Besides, I have a fine hunk of a man of my own anyway. This is just an excuse for all you save women to see some hard bodies on the sly," I told her. We laughed. She poured ginger ale into me and curled my hair. I applied my make- up and looked at myself in the mirror. I looked good. I got goosebumps.

The guests were arriving. I could hear Bria letting them into our hotel suite and pointing them toward the food and drinks. I went into the bathroom. I pulled out my cellular phone, but what I really wanted to do was crawl into the huge sunken Jacuzzi tub and let the jets shoot warm water into all of my muscles and knead me into a state of unconsciousness.

"Hi babe," Antoine answered. "I was just thinking about you. Shouldn't you be knee deep in bridal shower games and opening all those dirty gifts your girls really want to keep for themselves but can't because they don't have men?" He was cracking himself up. I laughed a little too. "That was last week. Tonight's party will be as raunchy as your little shindig," I said knowing this would shut him up. He wasn't laughing anymore.

"Hold on what... do you mean? Are you going to have strippers?" he asked.

"Aren't you going to have strippers?" I countered. He laughed a little less convincingly.

I had to get back to the party, so I told him, "I just called to say hi and have fun. Don't get into any trouble. I love you and I'll see you tomorrow afternoon."

My sick stomach and goose bumps were subsiding. "Okay Baby Cakes. We are meeting at the house for brunch at 11 right? Don't forget my mom will meet us there too," he said before ending our call.

The party was so much fun. We did play games but nothing like the ones we played with my grandmother, Mrs. Ethel, my First Lady, and friends from work. These games were outrageous. The male dancers were over the top too. My girl B was right, they were fine. The one who caught my eye the most whispered to me as he danced bare-chested around me.

"Is there anything about you that I should know?" he grinned and asked me softly. What a beautiful smile. And he smelled so good.

"Don't throw me up in the air or pull your business out or I will punch you in your pretty little face," I instructed and threatened. He laughed out loud, turned around and did a backbend in front of me. He did a flip and landed in a split. Then he beckoned for me to come to him. I bent over to hear the secret that he wanted to tell me, and all the girls started yelling.

He asked, "Can I touch you here?" pointing to my lady business, the part of my body where my thighs met.

"No" I quickly said and pushed his hand away. He pushed farther, "Can I kiss you?"

"Hell no," flew out of my mouth before I could stop it. "Can you kiss me then?" he asked while he puckered his lips. I tried to walk away but I bumped into another male dancer. He took my arms and put them around his neck. We swayed to the music. This was fine. Fun even. But then the real fine one started dancing behind me. I could feel his rock- hard penis pressing into my back. Not cool.

The girls were really going wild at the sight of me sandwiched between two hunks. Before I could protest the other two dancers were in the huddle with us. A pair of lips, luscious lips, but lips nevertheless, were coming toward me. I panicked and was about to start swinging. Strong arms swooped me up around the waist and carried me to the other side of the room. The girls and their dollar bills closed in on the rest of the half -naked men.

"Are you alright?" Mr. Handsome asked me. He placed me on my feet and helped straightened my denim-shorts jumper. I smoothed out my newly-curled hair. Why was he so damn fine? My stomach was queasy again, but I lied. "Yeah, I'm cool. What's your name?"

He said his name was Charles. He had just finished school to become a civil engineer. He was moving out of state to work for his uncle's firm in a few months. Until then he was dancing. "I danced on weekends while in college to keep some ends in my pockets. I am just doing it for fun now until it's time for me to go," he said.

I wanted to ask him a lot of other questions, but Bria grabbed my arm and pulled me aside. "Why are you interviewing the hottie? He is not an archeologist! And you are not at work. Do you have any CDs here? Theirs is scratched," she rattled off like she was a reporter. I went into the bedroom to find more music for the dancers.

After I handed Bria a CD, I stared at myself in the huge mirrored that covered the entire far wall. "What do you have against being touched?" Charles said startling me. He was standing in the doorway watching me look at myself in the mirror.

"I don't have a problem with it. As a matter of fact, I love it…as long as it is my husband who is doing the touching." I turned around and squared my shoulders to face him. I handed him another CD, one that Bria made for me to work out to. He smiled. His hand touched mine when he reached for the CD. His smooth skin was soft and warm.

"He is not your husband yet. When is the wedding?" Charles asked. I told him the details of my big day and noticed that my stomach was no longer upset. One of the other guys came in to change outfits, if you can call it an outfit. Little did I know that the routines would be performed with gradually fewer pieces of clothing. Charles noticed my chagrin and laughed again. He even has perfect teeth to match that smile.

"Hey," he called after me because I was heading back to the festivities. "I wish you the best of luck on your marriage. I hope you all take good care of each other. If ever you find yourself having to compromise your morals, values, or judgment…run, okay? It's no place for worst to go. It never gets better once it gets as bad as things can get," he said gently, as if he knew this first hand. Uh huh, I bet he would love for me to run right on over to him at Bellman Engineering of Atlanta, GA. He handed me his business card before closing the bedroom door behind him.

After the dancers, who had gotten all the way down to a very slight piece of cloth barely covering their very long, very hard, very thick penises, and after all of the wine, and all of the food, games, and gifts, Bria, Sheila, and I went to sleep. Actually, it was more like we passed out. It was seven a.m. when I drifted off to sleep. The pains in my stomach were back.

Chapter 11

There is no way that we could still get married!

If I looked half as bad as I felt, Antoine and his mother were going to run for the hills when they got a look at me. I showered, pulled my hair back into a ponytail, applied a bit of lip gloss, and flew out the door donned in a pair of blue jeans that suddenly felt too big and my St. Louis University t-shirt. I loved this t-shirt because it was a reminder that I needed to go back to graduate school and finish my master's degree. I decided I would go to school locally when I finished undergrad and Antoine proposed to me. I never got around to completing the coursework to earn my post-baccalaureate degree, even though both my grandmothers were urging me to. Even Antoine was encouraging me to get my Master's. He even called me Dr. Blanks and said I should go all the way and get a Ph. D after the wedding. Not many men did that.

I ran into the house intending to call out my future husband's name but choked on the words because of the stench in the air. What the …

I ran to the guest bedroom. The door was open, and he was not in there. I spun around in a circle a few times not knowing which way to go next. My feet moved me in the direction of our bedroom. The door was closed. I turned the knob. It was locked. "Honey, no don't do this." I pleaded. "You don't need to do this. We have a whole wonderful future ahead of us. We are not having any money problems. It's all good. Come on, stop it. Please," I was almost crying.

"Go away Karen. I don't want you to see me like this. Just go to the mall or something. My wallet is on the kitchen counter. I'll be okay in a little bit," Antoine said. He sounded sick, like he had a sore throat.

"Are you crazy? I'm not going anywhere. Don't make me do something we will both regret!" I barked. At first, I felt like I imagine one would feel when trying to talk a loved one out of committing suicide. Very quickly however, the soothing calm fled. I was angry.

"Open this damn door Tony. We both know what you are doing in there. Why the hell are you hiding?" I yelled. He told me to go away again. I said, "Okay you asked for it," and walked away.

"Don't call your grandmother! Please Karen, don't call Mrs. Toni over her with that gun. Karen!" he screamed through the door. I was in the kitchen pantry looking for the electric screwdriver.

I came back to the door that separated my drug using fiancé from my foot that was itching to implant itself in his behind. "Girl, what are you doing?" he bellowed when he heard the screw driver electrically making its way onto the other side of the door. He shocked me by suddenly cracking the door open a bit, just enough to see his face. "Babe, give me thirty minutes. I promise I'll let you in then." I swung the power tool toward his face and he slammed the door shut again. I kept working. I could hear Antoine bustling about in our bedroom. When the door was hanging on by just one screw, I kicked it in the rest of the way. I wanted to catch him red-handed. Until then, I had never actually seen him with my own eyes smoking crack. Why was it so important for me to see it? I also kicked in the door for dramatics. I needed him to know I meant business.

There he was. Carelessly but fully dressed. Erect penis sticking out of his pants. Vaseline, lap top, pornographic flick on the 17.5-inch lap top screen, several little white chunks of what looked like soap in an open plastic bag, and a cloudy glass pipe in his hand that moments before he held between his lips. I only know what happened next because it was later told to me.

I screamed as loudly as I could, knocked the laptop onto the floor, grabbed the bag of rocks, kicked Antoine in the knee, the one I knew he hurt while running track in college; and ran to the bathroom. Antoine was on my heels, still with his precious pipe in his hands. I opened the lid to the toilet and he grabbed my hand. "No Karen!" he said through tears. "Please, no."

I struggle to break free from him. He was very strong but was still no match for my determination to flush the drugs down the toilet. We wrestled. I fell. He fell on top of me. Even high he was concerned about hurting me. I used the brief second that he took to see if I was alright to lift my arm to the toilet and dump the imperfectly round rocks into the water.

We both froze. I thought he would go crazy and begin beating me up. He didn't. The pipe fell from his hands and hit the floor. The shattering sound sent us scurrying from our heap on the floor. I didn't want the drug filled pipe pieces to cut me. I stood up and flushed the toilet.

A deep, low, almost unreal sound emitted from my true love. It started as a moan, then crescendo into a wail. I was so afraid. I wished I would have called my grandmother now. This man was crying and reaching for me. I wanted to embrace him, but I was skeptical. Would he choke me to death for destroying his high? "Thank you, Karen," he said.

"Thank you, Baby. Oh my God, I would be dead by now if you hadn't stopped me. Do you know how much product that was?" he said. Product? He acted like we were discussing laminate tile or something normal. This was not normal. We sat back down on the bathroom floor of our master suite and held each other. We both cried. My stomach was in knots and I felt like I had to move my bowels.

After a few minutes he asked me to call his mother and make an excuse for him. "Tell her we will take her to lunch in a few days… before the wedding, okay Baby Cakes?" he instructed. Wedding? Was he crazy? There is no way we could still get married.

Antoine spent the next few days in bed. I stayed very close to him, but we did not interact like regular engaged to be married in a few short days couples would do. I worked on my lap top on some articles for next month's issue of the magazine that I worked for. I put food and water on his bedside table. He would not eat but drank everything I gave him. When I spoke to his, mother, I told her everything. Almost everything.

"Is he still doing that mess?" Antoine's mother asked me like the enabler that she is. "I thought he got his sense about himself when he was young. I didn't know he was still getting high," she defended. After a long pause she asked, "What is the primo anyway?" I didn't have the heart to tell her the real truth- that her son was now smoking straight cocaine. That was such a socially lower drug, and the mere mention of it meant the bottom of the gutter to most people. I continued the white lie, "It's a joint or blunt laced with coke. He said he has been doing it since he was a kid."

"He a lie! I would have known if my child was on a primo!" she denied. "It wasn't until that devil brother of his started coming around that he started that mess. I knew he was a bad influence, but what was I supposed to do? His own mama threw him out into the streets. She called him a fag and a dope head. I think he *messed with* my son. Lord have mercy on my poor boy!" Mrs. Blanks cried.

Oh Lord, have mercy indeed. This was an enabler if ever I saw one. I liked Mrs. Blanks, but she was very fragile. I could not have a reasonable conversation with her about this.

On Thursday, Antoine finally got up and got cleaned up. We were supposed to take his mom to lunch and have rehearsal at the church. My grandmother refused to go. She dryly said, "So, you are going through with these shenanigans, huh?" She had hoped that I wouldn't. I never told her about all the times I caught Antoine getting high, watching porn, and jacking off. She would have killed me him for doing that to me and killed me for allowing it. I also did not tell her that I was thinking about not going on with my plans to marry 'That Boy'.

Chapter 12

I wanted this to be a joke from Punked' and not my real life.

"Antoine, we need to talk," I began.

He started explaining immediately, "Look Babe, I know what I did was wrong. I don't even know why I did it. We were at the bachelor party one minute having a blast. We partied. Drank. Watched the girls strip, then somebody pulled out a bag of weed. I declined even though I caught a lot of grief from the fellas. But I kept thinking about you. Then coke lines appeared out of nowhere. I knew I needed to get away from it. I told them I had an early appointment with you and my mom. I had to go to bed. I shut myself up in the bedroom and left them to party until they passed out. This morning I got up and stepped over most of them and a couple of naked women and started driving home. The next thing I know, I'm in the old neighborhood. And well…" he said ashamed.

He continued, "I didn't smoke that much. Honest. You came in before I could, that's why I kept saying come back in a little while. I didn't have much time to get as high as I was trying to get." This was the most absurd thing I have ever heard.

"I don't want to get married Saturday," I admitted. He turned as grey as he was when getting high on crack when I said that.

We both sat silent for what felt like an hour. He just stared out into space. I felt drained and lifeless. My stomach had not stopped hurting and I really was pooping up a storm. I could barely eat either. I don't know if my wedding gown would have fit properly anyway. I had lost so much weight. Antoine's chuckles startled my consciousness and I returned to the present.

"You should have seen yourself with that screw driver! And when you were tussling with me to get those rocks down the toilet, whew! You were a little mini Toni Edmonds! All you needed was a .32," he described. I was tickled thinking about how I must have looked. This is when he told the story to me. He even acted out the parts and used his pseudo girl voice to imitate me. I don't know why I was laughing. Maybe because I wanted this to be a joke from Punked' and not my real life.

At the end of his rendition of my antics, he put his arms around me. "Karen, no one has ever loved me as much as you do. No one has ever loved me as hard as you do," he said. I began to cry. "You would never hurt me or allow me to hurt myself. Even when I mess up, you still love me unconditionally. I can't throw that away. Please baby. Let's go to the rehearsal. We have all these people lined up and waiting. Then, let's go to a N.A. meeting. We can take my mom out to eat another time. You know she really doesn't what to go anyplace any way. Then you can think about what you want to do over the next two days. If you decide not to marry me on Saturday, I will be the one to go to the church and tell Pastor and everybody it's off. But don't decide right now. Please Karen. Don't throw me away," Antoine said.

When we got to the church, everyone was there waiting. Pastor Greene said, "I thought the honeymoon was supposed to come AFTER the wedding. You two look like you have been in bed all day."

"It's all that partying they have been doing. They are still recovering from the weekend," Bria said before Sheila elbowed her in the side. Pastor laughed and mumbled, "Lord, do they really think I don't know what goes on at those parties?"

The church wedding planner called for everyone to get in their places. Bria and Troy stood at the alter with Pastor. I walked a third of the way down the aisle by myself. Then my grandmother was stationed to walk me a third down the aisle, and Mrs. Ethel was stationed at the last one third point and together the three of us met Antoine, who simultaneously walked to the alter from the choir stand behind the alter, at our respective places. No sooner than Pastor said, "Let us bow our heads for a word of prayer," did I faint.

I was positioned on a pew when I came to. A cool towel was compressed against my forehead. The first things I saw were my grandmother's worried eyes. I blinked back a few tears and she hugged me but instructed the others, "You all stand back and give her some room to breathe. How do you feel Love Bug?"

"I'm okay Grandma," I said more as a reassurance to myself than to her. I tried to get up. Antoine was immediately at my side. He took my hand and helped up. "Are you sure you are okay Baby Cakes?"

Bria and Sheila were just a yard away locked arm in arm nodding their heads as if trying to send an answer to me through osmosis. "Yes, yes. I'm okay. I guess I should have eaten breakfast this morning." I realized that Mrs. Ethel was sitting on the pew behind me when she said under her breath, "Maybe if you don't eat for the next two days you will pass out and stay out until the wedding is over." Pastor gave Mrs. Ethel a stern look and suggested we take a ten-minute break, so I could get a cold drink from the vending machine.

"Water is fine Pastor," I said noticing the church wedding planner had a glass in her hand. "Better get used to drinking tap water," my grandmother said not as lowly as Mrs. Ethel's shady remark. Then she added, "It may be all you can afford with his taste in clothes this one has," pointing to Antoine.

Antoine and I sat down. He was still holding my hand. Heckle and Jeckle sat very close to us. Antoine whispered to me, "Hang in there, Love Bug. You can take the next two days to think about how you feel."

"Don't call me that!" I spat. Did he really think that he could get on my good side by using my grandmother's nick name for me? The over-70 Peanut Gallery smirked.

Antoine inched down the pew a bit further, dragging me by the hand with him. He whispered even softer, "I love you Karen Angelique Edmonds. I always have, and I always will. You are the only woman in the world for me. I promise I will never, ever do that again. With you by my side, I don't need to get high. I won't hurt you anymore Baby. I promise."

The N.A. meeting was very moving. I was so emotional through the whole hour. The meeting was called to order. Visitors were acknowledged after a collective pledge was said. Everyone was so warm and friendly. I saw several people I already knew. An anonymous nod or a wink was all that was exchanged between us when they came my way for greetings. The stories that were shared by the circle of addicts and their guest were so powerful. I silently cried through the entire meeting. Even when the celebration of sobriety time began, I continued to shed tears, this time they were happy ones. "Keep coming back! It works!" they all shouted.

These men and women told stories of how they were in street ditches, literally, with no food, no money-nothing. Just a hankering for a high. But with God's grace and a lot of relapses, they made it through. Some of them have been clean for a year, five years, even fifty-five years. Wow! Amazing. People can really beat this thing, huh? And they all looked so normal. Some of them looked really good. In fact, the receptionist at my doctor's office was there and she always looked so good. The girl could dress her butt off.

A guy I went to school with was there. He was a lawyer and taught Criminal Justice at a local community college. He was handsome in a plain sort of way. I never would have guessed that he used drugs. These two people and many others there talked about how they overcame the gripping hold drugs had on their lives and how it was still a constant struggle to remain on the right path.

Antoine spoke next, "Good afternoon. My name is Tony and I am an addict."

Chapter 13

Woman! Give me the big girl version. Tell me the truth, the whole truth, and nothing but the truth.

Grandma always says, "Expect nothing." I can never remember a time when she was not there for me. Even when I did not even know what I needed myself, she anticipated my needs and provided for me in an instant. I have always been able to count on her. But I know that she does not count on anyone but herself. She does not trust people. I wonder what all happened in her life that made her so distrusting.

After our dinner. After the banana nut pound cake that Mrs. Ethel made for desert. After my phone call was made and grandma pretending that she was not trying to listen in. On the night that I moved back home for the last time, I wanted to delve more into the story that makes this 70-something year old woman think that she can relate to my man troubles.

"Grandma. how did you and grandpa meet?" I thought I should open with this safe story; one that I already knew a little something about.

"Oh, Lord!" Mrs. Ethel stated and got up to leave the room. Grandma began, "Child, why you wanna hear that old story again. I've told it to you a thousand times." This was true, but she has never told the adult me about it. It was always the candy-coated version that was more like a fairy tale for a seven-year-old.

"Woman! Give me the big girl version. Tell me the truth, the whole truth, and nothing but the truth." I had to put it to her the way I knew she would put it to me if the tables were turned.

She sat back in her chair and interlocked her fingers together. I was about to get a tongue lashing for speaking to her this way, or I was about to hear a very juicy, very different version of this story. "You hear this Ethel? My Bug-Bug wants the true story about me and Eddie." she yelled toward the kitchen. Mrs. Ethel fired back, "Tell her! It's time!" My grandmother sort of looked off into space and said:

> *I had been all mixed up with all kinds of no-good men when I finally left The Old Woman's house. First a cab driver who hit on me, then a married man who tried to rape me when I finally broke it off with him. The last fool talked me into stealing for him. He had me letting him in through the back door of this boarding house I worked at. For a room of my own, I cleaned and cooked for Mr. Wazenski and got to eat whatever I cooked too. That man was good to me, but my man, Davie, took his kindness for weakness. He said 'Leave the backdoor*

unlocked for me. You go on about your normal routine. Then when everything settles down, I'll sneak in real quiet and get one of them checks from Mister's ledger. I'll get one from the back, so he won't know it's missing.' Well, like a dummy, I did it. And it worked!

Grandma threw her head back and laughed. She clapped her hands and continued:

Davie wrote that check out for $25, more money than he had ever seen, and cashed it at the A&P. He told the store owner that he did some hauling and handy work for Mr. Wazenski. He even added, 'Mister say it's going to be more where that came from.' Well Bug, we lived high on the hog that weekend. Davie took me to a club, bought food and drinks, and even paid the club photographer to take our picture. There was a local Blues musician in the club that night, so Davie invited him to get in the picture with us. We sure did have a good time that night. I didn't know that kind of happiness existed.

It wasn't long before Davie wanted to do it again. I felt bad for poor Mr. Wazenski. He didn't deserve that. But, I left the back door open again. And again and again. And it worked again, except each time Davie was less and less attentive to me. On the last time he said he was going down to the pool hall to try to double his luck. When the bookkeeper realized that several checks were missing totaling $300, I was out of a job and Davie was picked up by the police and thrown in jail.

So, I was out on the street again. That is until I met Eddie, your grandfather. He was so pretty. Prettier than anybody- man or woman- than anybody I had ever seen before. And he had the biggest smile. Didn't take much to make him smile or laugh either. He just had a real easy-going spirit. Lord, he was dressed so nicely! I thought he was rich. But Eddie said he was in the police academy. I loved him instantly. We walked in the park and talked for hours. I told him about some of the fools I had been with. He said I needed some protection. Then he told me about this crazy girl he was going to marry before he wised up. I told him he needed some protection too.

He bought us some cold Cokes and we talked some more. It started getting dark and he asked if he could walk me home. Well, since I didn't have a home anymore, I told him no. I told him that I was more than capable of getting myself home. He laughed and said, "I've only known you for some hours Ms. Toni, but I can already tell that you are capable of doing anything that you put your mind to. I just want to spend a few more moments with you and if I can do that by walking you home then I wish you would let me.' Bug, we started walking and I did not know what I was going to do. After about three blocks he said, 'You sure were a long way from home. What is a pretty lady like yourself doing so far away from home?'

Tears just started running down my checks. We stopped and I told him the whole story about Davie and the checks. Eddie took me in his arms and said it would be okay. And for the first time in my life, it really was as okay as a man said it would be. He hailed a cab and took me two neighborhoods over. He got me a room in a house where he was also staying. I knew I could count on him.

He graduated from the academy and I was right there smiling from ear to ear. He asked me to marry him. After the wedding, we saved for a house. Barely nine months after we got the house was your daddy born. Then I had two beautiful, smiling men in my life.

Wow! Grandma really did have some crazy experiences with men. I never would have guessed her story was that wild. I had only heard about my grandfather, so I thought he was the only man she ever had. Mrs. Ethel was right – I do need to write a book about Grandma!

Chapter 14

I also know that I do not need his permission to react and remove myself for his hell,

This version of my grandmother's story left me wanting more. She said she had been slapped around, verbally abused, and "taken advantage of" by some others. "Grandma, you mean they raped you?" I almost yelled. A very forlorn look spread across my grandmother's face and she whispered, "It wasn't the first time I had been raped child."

My questions were flying out of my mouth without any pause for Grandma to answer them. Mrs. Ethel quickly re-entered the room from the kitchen that she claimed to be tidying up even though it was already clean. She took me by the elbow and helped me from the chair that I was already ready to pounce from. She expertly lead me to the stairs saying, "Let your grandmother gather her thoughts, Karen. Ya'll can talk some more tomorrow. Child, Toni can keep you busy for the next month telling you her story. But for now, you both need some rest."

Back in my room, the room that I grew up in, I felt a calming peace settle over me. At first it unnerved me. Why in the middle of an emotional storm do I feel calm? Then, I relaxed into it. I thought about the woman that my grandmother is today; I am the woman that I am today because of her. I am sure that I can tell her about my deeper man problems with Antoine. Compared to her former man troubles, my stuff was nothing. I also thought about the conversation I had with Antoine when I slipped away to call home.

During that conversation, I asked Antoine what he wanted. I needed to know where he wanted us to go from here. I know a lot of women would be done with the whole relationship. Many of my friends have left men for a lot less than what I have been through with Antoine, yet I am not sure what I want. I don't know if I still want to be with him or not. I don't know if the relationship can be salvaged. I love him. I have loved him ever since I was a little girl. Can a love like that last forever?

On the phone, he said that he needed some time. He wants to be together, but he admitted that he is not his best self right now. "I don't blame you for leaving Karen, I would have left me too," he said. I didn't know how to feel about that. I guess I'm proud that he accepts responsibility for his part in our problems. I also feel that he is a coward. I am not responsible for making him happy. Marriage is not supposed to make a man finally feel whole. I also know that I do not need his permission to react and remove myself from his hell, so I responded, "Well, that's very big of you Antoine. I just need to know why."

"Why do you do all of the stupid crap that you do? Help me to understand" I said this because I know that it is the only way that we can either move forward or move on without the other person. One way or another, we can't move until we clear the air.

I listened to Antoine for twenty minutes explain that he does not know why he does what he does. He said that it could be because his father did all of the same things. The senior Mr. Blanks abused alcohol and gambled. He watched porn. He frequented the nudie bars. And he cheated on his wife. "Antoine, have you ever cheated on me"? It's not like I didn't have reason for asking.

I was thinking back on one day when I went to Bria's house to get my hair done. She was a beautician in a well-known shop in the Galleria Mall and kept my hair healthy and stylish. She also had so many other clients, she often did hair in her home as well. By night she was training to become a personal trainer. She already had a few workout clients who had been members at the gym in the Delmar Loop that she used to attend. They quit going to that gym after meeting her because they could tell that she already knew what she was doing and joined her at her house. She already had a fully equipped gym in her basement.

Because of these two occupations, there was always someone at her home she purchased by herself by the time she was 21. I was glad to see a woman leaving in her 2015 black Range Rover as I pulled up in my 2017 black SUV of the same make and model. "Love your hair," I stated out my window. "Thanks girlfriend. Love your ride," she stated right back at me.

Bria was still standing on the porch by the time I got out of my vehicle. "Her hair was slamming," I said. "Thanks, Sis. She is a model and a dancer, so I can charge her Beverly Hills prices. Plus, she refers all the other dancers to me. You want me to hook your hair up like that too? You all are already driving the same SUV," Bria said. Maybe that's what I needed, a make-over.

"Yeah, but not tonight," I told her. "Oh, you want to go to bible study together?" she asked while reaching for her purse and keys. "No, I need to talk tonight," I told her. Girl when have we ever not been able to talk while you were in my chair? Come sit down," she instructed. She was so right, but tonight I needed her undivided attention. So instead we shared a half gallon of Reece's Peanut Butter Cup ice cream and I told her all about Antoine. She was in shock. She didn't say anything at first except, "Oh my God."

Once my dear friend got herself together and all of the information I had just unloaded on her sank in, she spoke. "First of all, Antoine is a good man. So, this issue is not bigger than he is. And he is also a saved man. So, God's got his back. Antoine is smart, and he is not going to let anything ruin him or your marriage. You keep praying and I'll be praying too. Now, let's get our butts down on the floor and do 100 crunches."

I did feel better after our short workout. I also relinquished and let her give me a new hair doo. She bonded in some longer straight human hair on the sides to give it an asymmetrical look. She added highlights and flat ironed it which framed around my face so perfectly that I did not want to lay down on it. It was very late when I got home so I sat on the couch in the living room and stared at, not watched the television.

I guess I started dozing off because I did not even hear Antoine when he walked into the room nor feel him when he sat next to me.

"Hi Babe," he said and kissed my cheek. Before I could respond, he snatched away and almost yelled, "What did you do to your hair?!"

"You like it Pooh?" I didn't want to fight anymore. I wanted to be happy for a long time. He just looked at my head with his mouth twisted. "It's fine, but it's not really you. I like your hair the way it was," he stated. So much for my makeover.

This hairstyle wasn't very different from my usual one anyway except for the color and extra length. I guess I would leave this style for the models and dancers. I pulled my hair back into a ponytail and we went to sleep.

"What happened to your hair?" Sheila asked when I got to work. "How did you know about my hair?" I asked puzzled. "Bria told me last night after you left her house," Sheila explained. Oh no, had Bria told Sheila about Antoine?

"Oh, what else did you and B talk about?" I asked. "Just about her doing my hair today and a diet and exercise routine for me. I need to lose about 30 pounds for the wedding," she said with a big smile on her face.

"Damon proposed?" I asked excitedly forgetting all about if my friend betrayed my trust. "No, but I told you I am getting married next year, with or without Damon," she said still smiling. I said, "I'm not quite sure how that works Sheila."

"Watch me," she instructed.

"Are you sure you even what to be married? This is really hard," I admitted. "Awww, is the honeymoon over already?" she asked mockingly. We laughed. I guess she did not know that I was married to a man with a crack, porn , clothes, and shoes addiction.

"Anyway, you don't need to be walking around looking like no stripper," she added. "I did *not* look like a stripper thank you very much," I told her as I crossed my arms defiantly.

"B said she styled your hair just like the stripper you saw coming out of her house last night," Sheila explained. Bria told me she was a *dancer*.

***

Later, I made an appointment with my ObGyn just to be sure I was not pregnant. This stomach thing was getting the best of me. We were not planning to start a family for a few more years. I hoped we had not messed up that plan. I really did want to go back to school. Things had picked up with Antoine at work, but I still prayed that I was not pregnant. I would hate for the prospect of having to take care of another person to throw him into another cycle of drug episodes.

We had been married for seven months. Things were good. I did not tell Antoine that I had an appointment with my doctor. I went to the doctor on my lunch break. I got the results of my pregnancy exam and couldn't wait to tell grandma that I was not pregnant. I stopped into my favorite sushi bar in south St. Louis to grab something quick to take back to the office. I stood in line at the take-out counter behind a tall dark handsome man in a tailored dark blue suite. I could tell that even from the back he was very well groomed and polished. He was also wearing a wonderful scent.

"Is that good?" I heard him ask the girl behind the counter. She must have been new because I had never seen her before, and she looked very perplexed at his question. I jumped in to help because I was very hungry and needed to hurry them along. All of the excitement about my negative pregnancy test had given me quite the appetite.

"The California Rolls and Asian salad are to die for. You should get that." He turned and flashed me his gorgeous smile. "Karen!" he exclaimed.

"Charles, what a surprise," I said. We hugged like we were old friends. "How have you been?" He asked. "Great! How about you?" I fired right back. He said, "Busy. My uncle is keeping me very involved with the company. We are expanding and I'm here scoping out office space." He looked even better in his crisp white shirt, sterling silver cuff links, and navy suite. I love a man in a suite.

"You look like you have lost weight." He reached out to touch my cheek. I turned away. "Oh yeah, I forgot, you will only be touched by your husband. He is your husband now, right.?" He asked. Was that a little bit of hope in his voice?

"Right, Charles. Don't get punched in the face," I reminded him playfully. He laughed. What a nice laugh.

"Seven months. All is well," I added.

"You have a minute to sit down and catch up with an old friend?" he asked. Charles was hardly an old friend, but I was too full of positive emotions to go back to work right now.

"Sure. Grab us a table and I'll step out to call my office," I said. Charles talked about his family's business, his apartment and neighborhood, and how he was struggling to find time to hit the gym. He was no longer dancing but wanted to remain in shape. He must have found *some* time because he still looked good.

He told me that he had gotten back with his ex-girlfriend, even though she had broken his heart last year by cheating on him. "I can tell already that it's not going to work out for us," he added. I felt kind of sad for him. Then he went on, "Once trust is broken, it's nearly impossible to get it back." I now understand how he knows first-hand about where *worst* can go.

Then he turned the conversation to me. I don't know why but I told him about my pregnancy scare. He suggested I see my internal medicine doctor soon.

I told him about the hairstyle I tried. He said he could not imagine any style looking bad on me. "He didn't say he did not like it. Just that he didn't like it on me," I tried to clear up. "Maybe he saw the style on the stripper in the club." Now how in the world did Charles know about my husband going to the strip clubs?

"Excuse me?" I must have said with a little too much attitude because he quickly explained, "You said the girl you saw it on was a dancer, right?" Of course. That had to be it! Antoine has been in the strip club and he knew this girl. Why didn't I think of that?

I raced home to confront Mr. Not Satisfied With The Woman He Has At Home.

"Karen, where is this coming from?" Antoine asked.

"I thought about it, Antoine. It makes sense doesn't it?" I asked.

"Yes. It does, okay it makes sense. That is exactly what it was. I have seen Candice at the club. She danced for me a couple of times. Flirted with me a bit, but I always told her I was not interested," he tried to explain to my back. I was out the door and in my truck.

"Karen! Karen! Wait a minute. Where are you going?" he tried to continue talking.

Chapter 15

No person should ever be allowed to destroy another person that way

I was surprised by Antoine's answer to my question about cheating when we talked on the phone the night I moved back to Grandma's house. It was so pure and so raw. The love of my life laid it all out before me as if it was the gospel according to the book of Mark. He said, "I thought about cheating... many times. I wanted to; especially when things were bad between us. But I never did. I knew I could not run the risk of losing you. Or worse, breaking you. I could never live with myself if I did to you what my father did to my mother. Karen, my mother is not in there," he said, and I pictured him tapping on his temple.

He continued, "She wasn't always like that. But he broke her. Broke her spirit. Broke her mind. Broke her womanhood. No man. No person should ever be allowed to destroy another person that way. I am sure that is what killed him - the guilt of knowing that he destroyed another person. I believe in my heart that he is burning in hell now for what he did to my mother."

Listening to Antoine reminded me of one of the other many sad stories that Grandma told me during the time that I stayed with her. I think that she felt that it was therapeutic for me to hear about her past life. The life that I never knew about before.

Sure, she would say a little something about the Old Woman this or the Old Woman that, but the details were astounding. She admitted that the woman who raised her tried to break her after my grandfather left them all to be with another woman. Grandma said that her father leaving, and the old woman's abuse almost killed her; but what happened between her and her sister was the catalyst for the broken period of her life.

We were sitting on the porch at dusk. Each of my grandmothers were on separate porch swings and I was sitting on the steps of our front porch. They were being warmed by the large mugs they held as they savored the after-dinner black coffee. I was already too warm and enjoyed a glass of ice tea as I also fanned myself with an old church fan I found in the kitchen drawer. We were all pretty quiet that evening. Grandma must have taken my silence as sadness. She began this tale much the way she did so many of the others.

> *"You know Love Bug, of all the pain I endured during those years of living with The Old Woman, I thought none of it was as bad as when my daddy left us. Oh my God, my heart hurt! But I was wrong. Lord, was I wrong! The pain of losing Agatha almost cost me my life," grandma began.*

I, of course, had questions already that I just could not hold. "Lost her?" I asked. "Where did Grace go, Grandma?"

"At first, nowhere physically. But later…"

Grandma's voice trailed off. She just stared into the darkening sky. I looked at Mrs. Ethel questioning with my eyes. This patient grandmother shook her head slightly and lowered her eyes. This was my cue to be quiet and wait.

My grandmother talked for what seemed like hours. Each time that I had questions, Mrs. Ethel would give me that look that said to just wait; the answers were coming. And they always did. Grandma told her story and as if she knew what I wanted to ask, stopped every now and then to clarify.

> *After Daddy left, The Old Woman was even more cantankerous than ever. She beat me with a wet bath towel when I accidently dropped mine into the tub of bath water. She threw a bowl of hot soup on me because I was so hungry, I tried to eat the soup as soon as she put it in front of me. She sat it on the table and said, 'Blow it Stupid.' Well, I blew it once and tried to eat it as fast as I could. I winced from the burn of the soup on my tongue. The Old Woman had a habit of taking food away from me and clearing off the table before I could finish, so I developed the habit of eating quickly. Plus, she often wanted us to go to bed quickly so that she could receive gentlemen callers.*
>
> *When the soup burned my mouth and I cried out, The Old Woman spun around. She grabbed my bowl and hurled the hot soup all over me. Agatha laughed. She had never laughed before at what The Old Woman did to me. Usually, my little sister was just glad that she was not the object of The Old Woman's fury.*
>
> *Yes, Agatha was hit on sometimes, but never like I was. The Old Woman burned me with her cigarettes. She hit me in the head with whatever she held in her hands at the time. She kicked me in the backside, even sending me falling down a flight of stairs before. The worst that Agatha got was a slap across the face or a*

spanking on her backside, but with her clothes still on. I never got the luxury of keeping my clothes on for a spanking. The Old Woman even spanked me in front of one of her boyfriends and made me take off my pants. And she wonders why whenever she turned her head, those rascals were always coming on to me.

Well, after a few years of the hurt and pain of watching Agatha laugh at my torment, one day she stopped. She didn't even seem to notice the abuse I suffered any more. One time she even stepped over me lying in the middle of the floor after a particularly bad beating. She didn't whisper 'What happened Sister?' or 'We are going to kill her one day, Sister.' like she used to. She even used to say, 'We are going to leave this place and M'dear ain't going to ever find us.' But that all changed. I lost my sister. She wasn't the same person any more. I don't know what The Old Woman did with my Aggie Pooh, but this was no longer the sister I knew. I felt so alone then. I seriously considered taking my own life.

Agatha started smoking, which was okay with The Old Woman. My sister would light The Old Woman's Pall Mall cigarettes on the stove and bring them to her. Before she would reach The Old Woman, she would take a few drags herself. When Agathe started showing up at home with cigarettes of her own, The Old Woman not only said nothing, she often borrowed them from Agatha.

Then, Agatha got a boyfriend. He was a thug, and he made a lot of money from selling dope and whatever else he did wrong. When he would walk Agatha home from school, he would bring Gin, cigarettes, and hamburgers from a little place around the corner from our house where the waters skated to your car side to take your order. The Old Woman loved all three of these gifts and would let the boy come in.

At first, she let him stay awhile. Then he became Agatha's Spades partner in the card game The Old Woman would let her play when her own boyfriends would visit. Before you knew it, she would act like she did not know when the boy stayed overnight and slept with Aggie in our room. Oh yeah, Bug, that low down goon scoundrel would have relations with my sister right in the same room where I slept in the next bed beside them. He was a dirty dog and The Old Woman was too.

When the boy, what was his name Ethel? Roy? Troy? Elroy? Anyway, when he started giving The Old Woman money for the rent, she stopped pretending that she didn't know that he practically lived there too. I was out of a room and a bed to sleep on because the Love Birds started locking me out. The Old Woman would just say, 'Sleep on the floor in the hallway. You ain't nothing but an animal anyway,' and then laugh. Guess what? Agatha began laughing again. I didn't know what had happened to my sister. She was the only family that I had left.

Well, as time went on, Agatha started staying out all night. She was drinking and partying with her man. She started skipping school and The Old Woman didn't do a thing about any of it. She no longer verbally or physically hurt Agatha. Not even when a woman from the neighborhood came over and told The Old Woman that she saw Grace coming out of the big house on Laclede Lane where a Jamaican woman performed abortions.

While sitting in the window in our house, The Old Woman listened to this lady's account of how Agatha was crying, and her boyfriend had his arm around her as they left the abortion house. But The Old Woman told the lady, 'Shut up and mind your own business before I put a spell on you and your ugly daughters that no man wants no way!' Then she shook an old doll that we used to play with at the lady. The doll was missing its head. The Old Woman usually sat in the window with it and tapped on the window to scare away the birds. She scared the lady away by adding, 'If you repeat that to anybody, one of your kids will come up missing!' That woman scurried away from our window. When Agatha got home, nothing was done. The Old Woman didn't even say anything. Not even when

Agatha did not get up to go to school the next morning. Aggie didn't go to school for weeks.

Now I know it was wrong, but I was tired of Agatha not getting into any trouble. It got so that The Old Woman was even hitting me for the things that Agatha did wrong around the house. And I was really mad at Aggie for not going to school. We loved school. So, I asked The Old Woman, 'Are you going to whip Agatha for dropping out of school?' She just stared at me, then turned her back. I kept pushing, 'Are you going to get her for having that abortion?' Before I got the last syllable out of my mouth, The Old Woman slapped me with the back of her hand so hard that I literally saw stars. The next day, Love Bug, my Aggie Pooh was gone. I never saw my sister again.

After about a month, it was clear she was not coming back. I went into the bathroom and took all of the pills in all of the medicine bottles that were in the medicine cabinet. I never really knew why The Old Woman was prescribed so much medicine, but she never took them anyway. She found me on the bathroom floor. And that heif-, sorry, I mean woman poured a bucket of cold water on me. When that didn't help me, she drug me to the toilet and stuck her finger down my throat. I threw up for days after that. She never called the doctor or took me to the hospital. That old hag just kept giving me black coffee. I threw that up too. I didn't want to live anymore. Not without my sister.

Chapter 16

Funny how life turns.

I understand being broken. I understand experiencing pain that is big and deep and wide and long. What I do not understand, will never understand is allowing that pain to be the end of your story.

My grandmother got better. She allowed real love to heal her. She gave birth to her beautiful baby boy and lavished him with all the love she never received as a child. And when he had a child, her heart burst with love all over again. I learned how to love unconditionally from my grandmother. And I would teach Antoine this very important lesson.

I stayed with Grandma for a while even though I was now a married woman. We did move forward with the wedding; however, Antoine and I were in counseling together and separately. We were also going out on dates together. Grandma and Mrs. Ethel thought that this was silly of course, but Grandma could not put up much of a fight because that fall and winter, she was fighting a lingering cold that took away all of her strength. She slept a lot, which had me very worried.

"Don't go fussing and worrying Karen. We are old. It's normal for us to begin breaking down and slowing down," Mrs. Ethel tried to convince me. We were in the kitchen making grandma some homemade chicken soup and fresh squeezed orange juice. She did not have an appetite, but Mrs. Ethel insisted that grandma at least try to eat a little bit of food every few hours.

"Grandma, I am taking you back to the doctor in the morning," I said to her before tucking her into bed one night. Funny how life turns. She has been tucking me into bed all these years, now suddenly I am the parent and she is the child. "Okay, Bug. Okay," she replied before closing her eyes and drifting off to sleep. I thought that she would put up a fight because she had been to the doctor twice already. The doctor said that it was just a little cold, but it seemed much bigger to me.

The next day I took off from work, sent Antoine a text to let him know that I would not be able to go to our counseling appointment, and called Mrs. Ethel. "I'm going with you," grandma number two tried to say quickly. I guess she thought if she could slide this in and then get off of the phone real fast, that I wouldn't object.

"Oh no! No way. I can only handle one of you at a time and the one that must go is sick, so I will already have my hands full with her," I insisted. Traveling with two older people is almost as bad as traveling with two small children. I have to be sure that they are both safe and have everything that they need; and none of the things that they do not need. This duo was usually especially tiresome for me because they usually had so much energy. I would feel like a limp noodle after taking them to the grocery store or farmer's market. I was too concerned about Grandma to be concerned about anything else today. I needed all of my energy.

I told Mrs. Ethel that I could get in and back home quicker with just Grandma. She finally admitted that this was probably true and agreed to stay home. She added, "I'll stay over there, Bug until you all get back. I'll get the dinner started and clean Toni's room." I could hear the worry in her voice. She also sounded a little nervous, but continued, "I'll also do the laundry. As long as I have known Toni-Girl, she has never had many things in the dirty laundry basket. I was over there yesterday with her while you were at work and her clothes were spilling over. I was going to put them in the wash then, but she said leave them. She wanted to just continue to sit and talk instead. Poor Toni." Mrs. Ethel's eyes were filled with tears. Now I was even more worried.

***

While waiting for the doctor to see Grandma, I looked up from a copy of a magazine that featured one of the articles I had written this month, to find a handsome man standing before me. He said my name as if he knew my soul. It was Antoine. He said that he went by our house after he read my text about not making it to counseling. He said he knew that something was really wrong. Mrs. Ethel told him we were here. I was surprised to see him, but even more surprised that Thelma told him where Louise and I were. He sincerely added, "I can't imagine Mrs. Toni sick, so I got concerned and wanted to be here for you both." I said that was very sweet, but before I could say more, the doctor was ready to see Grandma. So, I said, "See you in a bit," and helped Grandma walk toward the smiling nurse in the pretty purple scrubs.

After a thorough exam, a lot of blood work, a shot of Tamiflu, and even intravenous fluids, Grandma's doctor said that she wanted to admit her into the hospital for observation overnight. I don't know why, but I instantly started crying. Both Grandma and the doctor tried to console me at the same time.

"Oh, Love Bug, it's going to be alright. Don't cry. I'll be home tomorrow good as new. Now, dry your eyes Karen and stop your worrying," grandma said while the doctor was also saying, "It's okay, Mrs. Blanks. These things are pretty common with our Silver Citizens. I'm sure everything will be fine."

I liked that Dr. Hruz called her patients Silver Citizens. I liked that they were both softly rubbing my arms to help sooth me. But I did *not* like the queasy feeling bubbling up inside of my stomach.

Chapter 17

Lord, how often will my brother sin against me, and I forgive him?

I went home alone, and for the very first time ever, I slept in my grandmother's house...the home I grew up in...all by myself. I felt so small. Every sound that the house made was amplified in my ears like a brand-new Bose system. I could even hear things outside and down the street. I missed my grandmother dearly. Please Lord, take good care of her and heal her. Let her come home good as new.

I couldn't sleep, so I got out of my bed and went into my grandmother's room. Grandma was so neat. Everything had a place. Her bed was made, and all her clothes and shoes were put away. Her bible was neatly laying on her bed-side table. I opened it to where there was a white feather holding the last place that Grandma was reading. Matthew 18:21-22 says, "Then Peter came up and said to him, 'Lord, how often will my brother sin against me, and I forgive him? As many as seven times?'" I stopped. This seems to be the theme of my grandmother's life. According to the stories she was telling me about her father, past boyfriends, the old woman who raised her, and her sister, Agatha; Grandma had to have forgiven them in order to be the graceful woman who is so full of mercy that she is today. She had to have healed from all of that pain in order to be happily married for so long. She had to have learned all too well what Matthew 18:21 really meant in order to remain best friends with the same person for her whole life long. She had to literary be in search of grace, and found it, in order to love me as she does.

I continued to read The Book of Matthew. "Jesus said to him,' I do not say to you seven times, but seventy-seven times.'" Before I closed The Good Book, a picture fell out of the back of it. It was a picture of Antoine and me on our wedding day. I held it in my hands and thought about this day. The day that I had finally become Mrs. Antoine Jamar Blanks.

We did not get married on that Saturday when I discovered Antoine getting high after out bachelor/bachelorette parties, but instead told our family and friends that I was sick. We agreed to get married immediately after Sunday service the following week last year. It had been a very warm spring, so Bria and I decided to decorate the church in as many pastel-colored flowers as we could get our hands on. The heavenly scents helped to set the light mood that was in the air. Almost every member of the congregation remained for our ceremony. Neither Antoine nor I had a lot of family left and even fewer friends. I was glad when Mrs. Ethel suggested that we invite the whole church.

"Karen, I was watching an old movie last night and was reminded how long ago, the entire community attended your wedding. It made the occasion even the more special. You all should do that too. Tell Pastor to marry you right after church that way, everybody can be a part of your special day," she stated. Even I had to agree that it was a marvelous idea. It would make the pain in my heart less tense. I did not want to cancel the wedding so close to the date, but I also know that we needed help if we were to ever have a real marriage.

My dress was ivory and very soft. It was simple, but quite elegant. I wore my hair in a side ponytail of soft, flowing curls with a crown of flowers around my head. The flowers matched the flowers in the church and in my bouquet. Antoine wore a light beige linen suite and donned a soft pink pocket square. A teenager from the church played the cello as the other guests flowed in. The choir sang two of my favorite songs before our pastor performed the ceremony and one of Antoine's favorite songs after we were pronounced husband and wife. My two grandmothers, who were dressed to kill, walked me down the aisle and stood beside me as my matrons-of-honor. Antoine's mother stood with him. Through all of the planning, we all called her his Best Mom. The whole day was simply beautiful.

We didn't have any other bride's maids or groomsmen. At the alter was just Pastor Greene, Antoine, his mother, my two grandmothers, and me. But I felt another strong presence in the midst. I knew God was with us and His Holy Spirit was in us. All of the trials and tribulations that we have faced over the years were worth getting to this place finally. Together. I had never known joy like this this before. I had also never known pain like the pain that has followed since our nuptials. It has been a roller coaster ride.

***

Now, after taking Grandma to the doctor, I stayed up all night and half the morning looking at my wedding photos. I even found my grandmother's copy of our wedding video and watched it over and over again. Eventually I fell asleep on the couch in front of the TV. My dreams that night were more vivid than they had ever been.

I dreamed that some men in white doctor's coats came and took Grandma from our house. I was crying and yelling, but Mrs. Ethel kept telling me just say the magic words and Grandma will come back. I kept asking her, "What are the magic words, Mrs. Ethel?" but each time that she started to tell me, Jesus would appear and say, "Forgive him." Then Antoine appeared and the clothes I was wearing suddenly changed to my wedding gown, complete with flowers on my head and in my hands. He smiled at me and said, "There! Now we can go and get Mrs. Toni from the hospital."

I woke to the sound of the kitchen telephone ringing. I remembered that my grandmother was in the hospital and jumped up to answer it fearing that her doctor was trying to get in touch with me. After running into the big chair near the couch and slipping on the area rug, I reached the phone just in time to hear the caller hanging up. I felt a stabbing pain in my stomach, then I felt sick as if I needed to throw up. Reluctantly, I checked the caller I.D. I hoped it was not bad news. As I hit the button to call back the number, I prayed that when Dr. Hruz picked up, she would say I could come to take Grandma home.

"Hi, I believe the doctor just tried to call me. This is Karen Blanks, Antonia Edmonds' granddaughter," I groggily said to the receptionist who answered the phone.

"Oh, good morning Mrs. Blanks. Yes, I just left a message on your voicemail for you to call us here in the office. I am sorry for waking you," she politely said. I could not tell from her voice if she had good news for me or bad. I quickly asked, "Is my grandmother alright?"

I wanted to scream and reach through the phone to shake the lady when she only said, "Hold on. I will let the doctor explain." Somebody better tell me something right now before I pass out.

Chapter 18

Whatever she had to tell me would not affect me.

My grandmother's bloodwork not only showed that she had an infection in her body, but also, there was a problem with her heart. More tests were needed. In the meantime, the doctor said that she ordered more fluids and an antibiotic. She also said that Grandma was asking for me. Of course, I informed the doctor, "I'll be right there."

I needed to throw up, but I couldn't. I tried so that I would be better once I got in front of my grandmother. She would know in a second that something was not right with me. I don't know if this keeps happening when I become upset or if something is wrong with me that my doctor missed. I am going to have to go back or get a second opinion soon. Once I get Grandma all better.

I walked into my grandmother's hospital room and froze in my tracks. My tiny little grandmother looked even tinier in the big hospital bed. She was hooked up to an oxygen machine and had tubes coming out of both arms. Miraculously, however, she was resting peacefully. I walked over to her and just stared at her beautiful little round face.

Grandma was a knockout. When she was younger, she could have any man that she wanted. But she didn't want any man. Grandma wanted a man after God's own heart. She always told me that this was the most endearing quality in a man. "Bug, you want a husband who loves God first. That way, he will love you best like your grandfather loved me," Grandma would always say.

I sat in the chair next to her bed and leaned forward in it. Without moving or even opening her eyes she softly said, "Hi there my Bug Bug." I laughed a little and asked, "How did you know that I was here?" She opened her eyes and looked over at me. She looked tired. Her eyes looked weak. "Because I saw The Lord and I asked Him to send you in so I could tell you some things. I asked Him not to take me yet. I am not finished telling you all that you will need to know in order to be all that you can be," she said.

Before I could say that it was not time for her to go to heaven yet anyway, she said, "Don't you know that My Father said that He was not taking me right then anyway." Then she chuckled a little bit. My heart almost broke in two. "Of course not, Grandma," I said. "You are still much too young to…"

When my voice trailed off, grandma knew that I couldn't even bring myself to even say the word. She rescued me the way that she had my entire life. "Karen, I need to tell you something," Grandma said. "I need to tell you something about your mother. Something I never told you before," she added. Something told me I did and did not want to know.

Grandma reached for my hand. I held her hand with both of my hands. She looked uncomfortable at the prospect of telling me whatever it was that she had to tell me. I wanted to take away some of the sting. I love my grandmother and I never wanted her to hurt. Besides, she was the only mother that I had ever known. Whatever she had to tell me would not affect me. She began,

> *We were all so happy when my son told me he and his new wife were expecting a baby. He came busting through my front door with the biggest smile on his face that I had even seen before. I had just come in from work. My feet and back hurt too bad to even fix myself some dinner. Ethel was on her way over with some meat loaf, green peas, and mashed potatoes. Once Kenny said, 'Ma, Carolyn and I are going to have a baby!' I forgot all about my aches, pains, and empty stomach. We laughed and cried and hugged each other tight.*
>
> *Then I called over to Ethel's. She answered the phone, 'Toni Mae, I'm coming, I'm coming!' All I could say is, 'We're having a baby! We're having a baby!' I think she dropped the phone or maybe she put it down because I never heard her hang up. All of a sudden, she came busting through the door just like Kenny had done only minutes earlier.*
>
> *Ethel was screaming and jumping all around. Your daddy and I joined in with her and before you know it, we were a trio of jumping, laughing, crying, fools. Bug, I tell you it was as if you were going to be the first baby ever born. We were so happy for Kenny and with him.*
>
> *You took forever coming here though. It was the longest nine months ever. But finally, the day came when your daddy called to say that he was taking your mother to the hospital. She was in labor. I called Ethel screaming, 'It's time Ethel Girl!'*

We got in my car and drove so fast to the hospital. When we got there, people knew who we were too. We came flying through the emergency room doors saying at the same time that we were there to have a baby. The nurses all pointed to where your mama was sitting in a wheelchair and your daddy was down on one knee in front of her as if he was proposing again. No sooner than we saw them did the nurse call Carolyn's name. All three of us started walking toward the door, then we heard your mama say, 'Can I go too?' Oh, how w laughed!

The nurse made Ethel and me stay in the waiting room. After a few hours, they sent us up to the maternity ward's waiting room. Our baby had arrived. Ethel and I held hands like two young school girls. We walked quickly and talked even faster. I said, 'I know it's a boy. Kenneth Edmonds Jr.' Ethel was just as sure that we were having a boy. She kept saying, 'Lil Kenny. I like the sound of that. Lil Kenny.'

The nurse came into Grandma's hospital room and asked Grandma how she was feeling. Grandma said that she was fine and introduced me to the nurse. "This is my granddaughter, Karen. She is the apple of my eye." The nurse smiled and shook my hand. Her name tag read, "Cheryl" and she had very warm hands. She said, "Nice to meet you, Karen. Your grandmother has told me and the other nurses all about you. I hear you are a writer." Grandma was always bragging on about me.

After seeing that Grandma was okay and that I did not need anything, the nurse left the room. Grandma continued her story.

Well Bug, needless to say we were quite surprised to walk into your mother's Hospital room and see your daddy holding a tiny pink blanket-wrapped baby girl. Ethel practically floated in singing, 'A girl, Toni! We have a baby girl!' But my feet wouldn't move. Still standing at the door, I began to cry. My son looked so proud standing there with his daughter in his arms. He handed you over to Ethel like you were a fine piece of delicate crystal belonging to the Queen of England.

Ethel started talking in a high-pitched baby voice saying how beautiful you looked, "Hello baby girl. My, my, you are so beautiful."

*Kenny walked over to me and put his arms around me. He asked, 'What's wrong, Ma? Are you upset that she's a girl?' Bug, I was moved beyond words. I thought that I wanted another boy in the family. I never thought that God would give me such a precious gift as a grand**daughter**. My heart grew so big. I thought it would burst. Kenny got the baby from Ethel as I fixed myself in the chair next to Carolyn. I blew her a kiss and said, 'Thank you.' That made her smile. When my son put his daughter in my arms, I cried even harder. Carolyn laughed even harder. They all did. I didn't care. I just kissed your little hands and feet. You were my Love Bug.*

It almost killed me when your daddy was killed in that accident a few months later. It almost killed your mama too. She would not eat or bathe. She stayed in the bed and cried every day. She never left the house. I moved ya'll in with me to take care of you both. Of course, you know Ethel had to help me.

Finally, Bug, your mama did begin leaving the house. Then she stopped coming back to the house. At first, she would stay out one or two nights a week. I thought that was odd but was glad that she was healing. One day Ethel and I were sitting on the porch and a car pulled up. The man inside the car yelled to us, 'Is Carol in there?' We just looked at him because we knew that he was a criminal from the next neighborhood over. When we didn't answer him, he yelled a curse word and peeled off down the street real fast. Ethel and I looked at one another and shook our heads. We knew that was the first sign of trouble.

When Carolyn finally came back home, I asked her about the thug who came by for her. She said, 'I met him at a party, and he brought me home one night when I had too much to drink." I warned her about him, but she insisted, "Mama Toni, Dion is alright. He is harmless." I asked around about where to find him when she didn't come home for a whole week. I left you with Ethel making her promise to take care of you if I didn't make it back home alive. My pistol and I went over to the area where I had heard Carolyn was hanging out and turning tricks in order to buy drugs. Some of the young people down the street said that she was a crackhead whore now and worked for Dion.

A doctor and a nurse came into Grandma's room. I wanted to yell, "Come back later!" but this unfamiliar doctor said that it was time to get Grandma's vitals again and talk to us about a procedure he recommended in order to take a better look at my grandmother's heart. I could hardly wait to hear the rest of the story, but first things, first.

Chapter 19

Baby, you are going to die if you keep this up.

"So, Grandma, what happened when you went looking for my mother?" I asked my grandmother as soon as the patient tech brought her back into the room and got her into the bed. She raised the head of Grandma's bed so that she could sit up. Once settled, Grandma continue,

> *I found your mama. She was in a vacant house with a bunch of strange folks all looking like the walking dead. I snatched her up by the arm, but some funny-looking character tried to stop me. As soon as he yelled, 'Hey! What do you think you're doing?' I pulled out my gun and yelled back, 'I think I'm taking my daughter home to her child! Do you mind?' He backed away quickly and all the rest of the zombies looked away.*
>
> *I got Carolyn to her feet and we made it to the car. She started crying and talking about her husband, being too young to be a window, and not being able to breath sometimes. I felt so bad for her, Bug. She was really a mess. When I pulled up to the house, I realized that I could not let you see her like that. I went to the door to make sure Ethel kept you from seeing us come in. I heard the car door slam behind me and when I looked back, your mama was running away down the street.*
>
> *Karen, I had to let her go. I knew enough to know that I could not help her if she did not want to be helped. I also knew that she would be of no use to you either. Not in her current condition. Well, I waited about another week and went back to that nasty crack house. There she was, on her knees in front of some mangy-looking critter. I didn't care, I went over and pulled her up from his crouch area. I told her, 'Listen, if this is the kind of life you want for yourself, so be it. But you will not live such a life for my granddaughter. This is my last time coming over here, risking my life to get you. If you leave again, then you might as well stay. Forever! You can forget that you have a daughter.'*

My mouth fell open. I think I even let out a slight whimper. I put my hands over my mouth to keep any more sounds from escaping, but nothing could keep the tears from fleeing my eyes and taking up residence on my cheeks. Grandma's eyes welled up with tears that threatened to spill too. She reached out her hand for mine, but I jumped as if I had just felt a burn. I stood up and asked, "What did she say? What did my mother do?"

> *She said, 'Then I guess I don't have a daughter.' Karen, she went back to what she was doing. The man started laughing and pulling on her dirty, matted hair. He also said, 'Get on away from here granny. And don't come back, right Carol?" I screamed, 'Her name is Carolyn! Carolyn damnit! And she has a beautiful little girl at home she needs to take care of!' Your mama looked up at me and said, 'Go on, Mrs. Toni. Get on out of here. Don't come back here anymore, okay?'*
>
> *But Bug, I did try again to help her. I told her, 'Baby, you are going to die if you keep this up.' Having satisfied her customer, she said, 'I'm already dead.' She got up and walked away. I could hardly believe that they went right on with their business, but he pulled up his pants and threw some money down on the floor, then he walked away. And Karen, wouldn't you know it; I tried one more time to get her to come home with me. I said, 'Kenny would not want you to live like this, Carolyn. Please, let's go home. We can get you some help.' I didn't even see where she went. I was just talking into the air. I was furious. Before I walked out, I said again, 'Don't you ever come back to my house Carolyn! You can forget that you have a daughter.'*

The realization that my grandmother told my mother that she could not be in my life anymore, hit me like a bus. I felt like I would melt into the floor. I wanted to. People could just walk on me, stand on me, and wipe their feet on me.

I remember when someone came to our house to tell Grandma that my mother was dead. Sadness crept over me like a shower. I remember feeling so hurt, but too afraid to show it. I didn't feel like I could ask anybody any questions. Grandma and Mrs. Ethel's reactions told me that it was a very delicate situation. Now that I look back on it, they were handling me. They said things like, "I know you think you should be sad, but really you didn't even know her. That's kind of good. It saves you a heartache." This was too impenetrable for a seven-year old to understand.

Now I understand all of the whispering. It makes sense now when Grandma would slip and say that she would not *let* my mama drag me through the mud. Each time I overheard her telling her partner in crime that she didn't let me live that kind of life back then and she certainly was not going to let me live that kind of life with Antoine, I thought she was just being a loving grandmother. Antonia "Toni" Rene Edmonds is more than what meets the eye. I wonder what other secrets she is keeping from me. I knew exactly who to ask.

***

I left the hospital to pick up Mrs. Ethel. I knew she was dying to get to the hospital to see about her best friend. She had called my cell phone a hundred times. I only answered once to tell her that Grandma was doing well and that I would come to get her soon. I let it go to voicemail all the other times. Once I could get her in my car all alone, she could talk to me as much as she wanted.

"What ever happened to Agatha?" I said as soon as Mrs. Ethel opened her front door. "Well, hello to you too," she said sarcastically. I kissed her cheek and watched her lock her front door. "Is that door over there locked?" she asked pointing to my grandmother's house.

"It has been locked since early this morning. Stop trying to avoid the question." I answered. Just then, my phone rang. It was Antoine. I knew I had better answer. He didn't mind blowing up my cell phone too.

The night that I found out that Antoine knew the stripper from Bria's house, Antoine called my cell phone at least fifty times. I listened to a few of the messages, but then stopped. I could not stand to hear any more of his nonsense. I was at my office and catching up on the work I should have been doing when I was out having lunch with Charles.

Charles and I exchanged business cards before leaving the restaurant. This time his card read "Partner/Civil Engineer." I told him I thought there may be some office space available in the building where the journal's offices are. I tucked his card into my desk drawer.

I worked well into the evening. I was a little disappointed that Antoine's calls stopped. I also felt guilty about storming out the way that I did and not responding to his calls. I missed him already. Reaching for the phone, I jumped when it rang in my hand. I picked it up and purred, "Hi Honey Bun."

"Well hello to you too My Love." This was not my husband. "What? Who is this?" I stammered. Charles laughed, and I instantly knew. I also instantly smiled. Why?

"What are you doing at work so late? I was about to leave you a message thanking you for lunch today," he said.

"Now see, that's how rumors get started. I did not take you lunch today, Sir," I corrected. "No, but you made an awesome recommendation and you were also terrific company," he admitted. I was smiling again. I was going to have to control myself.

"Well, in that case you are welcomed. Have a good night," I said. I heard him wish me a good night too before I hung up. I could not wait to get home to my husband.

On the way home, I called Bria and told her about Antoine knowing Candice. "Girl, everybody knows Candice. If she is not in a bikini at some car show or passing out the latest alcohol samples in some club wearing close to nothing, she is spinning around a pole. She got breast implants, compliments of her sugar daddy, just so she could be a Hooter's girl a few years ago. So, if a man eats chicken, drinks liquor, likes cars, or goes to strip clubs, they know Candice," Bria said. Sad.

***

I was not feeling much better. I had an appointment with my Primary Care Physician and besides being a little anemic, there was no reason for me to be feeling like I did. "Have there been any major changes in your life recently Karen," Dr. Holt asked me. "I got married," I said.

"I'm going to refer you to a Women's Health Group. They have psychiatrist who also specialize in the physical and emotional health and wellness of women," my doctor said. Great, so she thinks I'm crazy.

***

Anyway, I quickly told Antoine what was going on with Grandma. I told him that I had just picked up Mrs. Ethel and was headed back to the hospital. "I will call you when I get back home," I said.

"I'll see you there, Karen. I want to be there for you. You all are my family too," Antoine reminded me.

"Yes, I know, I said. "Okay, I'll see you there," he added. Then he said, "Is it okay if I bring my mom with me? She asked about Mrs. Toni, so I thought it would be nice if I brought her to see for herself." I was stunned, and somehow managed to say, "Yes, she is my family too." It was all that I could think to say. Actually, what I was thinking was, "Does she know that she has to leave the house to get to the hospital?"

Once we were in the car, seatbelts on, and car started, I asked Mrs. Ethel again, "Where is Great-aunt Agatha?" I expected her to say that Agatha was dead or lived very far away, but all she said was, "I don't know."

So, that means she could be alive. She could be right here in St. Louis. She could be somewhere in the world wondering where her sister is. I began to say this to Mrs. Ethel, but she interrupted by saying, "Child, didn't your grandmother tell you that Agatha ran off? She never saw her again. Why are you concerned about her?"

I told Mrs. Ethel that Grandma had told me about my mother. I told her that only a monster could keep a sick woman from her only child. I admitted feeling sorry for Grandma each time she told me a story from her past. I believed that she was a victim, but maybe there was more to the story. Something that she was not telling me. Something that would turn her into the kind of person that would tell a child not to hurt for her dead mother. Only Agatha could tell me what really happened. I had to find my grandmother's sister.

We got to the hospital to find that my grandmother's condition had worsened. She fell asleep and the nurses could not wake her up. She also seemed not be able to swallow. The doctor wanted to put her into a medically induced coma. All I could do was cry.

Antoine came in and swept me up in his arms. Mrs. Ethel sat on Grandma's right side and held her hand. The senior Mrs. Blanks stood on the other side and held Grandma's left hand. I was so afraid, but I told the doctors to do it.

Chapter 20

Whatever happened to Agatha?

Grandma remained in a coma for three days. Mrs. Ethel stayed there by her side all three days. Mrs. Blanks even visited every day. That all made me feel comfortable enough to go to work during the day. Antoine and I met at the hospital every evening. We all prayed and talked to Grandma. I believed she could hear us. I told her that I forgive her, but I still wanted to know more. I had so many questions.

Mrs. Ethel tried to fill me in; however, it was clear that she was still trying to protect my grandmother's image. She said, "Karen, your grandmother really should be the one to tell you this." I could not wait. Besides, what if Grandma didn't wake up? What if there was a problem with her brain or her speech when if she did wake up? "No, I want to hear it from a third and neutral party. Whatever happened to Agatha?" I asked.

Mrs. Ethel said that after Agatha had the abortion, she ran away from home. At first, they did not know where she was, but then her boyfriend came by and told The Old Woman that they were living in Madison, Illinois. He said, "I knew you would be worried about her and since I was over here on business anyway, I thought I should come by and tell you." This grandmother also said that they knew what kind of business he was in and that made them all worry about Agatha even more.

So, that's it. I need to go across the Mississippi River into Madison and find my great-aunt. But Mrs. Ethel said no. She said no sooner than Agatha's boyfriend told them that, then Agatha ran away from him too. He said that he did not know where she was. I was disappointed to hear her recall that, but I decided to use the Internet to try to find her. I had to get to the bottom of my grandmother's life story. I believe this would help me understand how Grandma turned into the kind of person who would take my mother away from me.

I had to know if my mother was forced to stay out of my life or if she would have cleaned herself up and come back for me if allowed. Was Grandma the kind of monster to stand in the way of mother and daughter?

Grandma was in the hospital another two days after coming out of the induced coma. She was fine, thank God. She said that she felt much better. I used the time that she was at St. Mary's Hospital to do some research. Antoine came over every evening and helped me. He said that this was our date night and counseling session rolled into one. He has been clean for months. He also said that he was ready for us to get back together and work on our marriage under one roof. I was ready too.

When I found what I believed to be my grandmother's sister's address and phone number in Chicago. I wanted to call the number immediately, but Antoine said, "Let's just drive up there. That way if it's really her, she can't hang up on you." I agreed.

We got Grandma settled in when she came home from the hospital. Of course, she wanted to get busy doing stuff around the house and in her garden. My grandmother loved her garden. She had herbs, peppers, onions, and okra. She said working in the dirt made her feel close to God. I never understood that, but I loved working right alongside of her.

I put Barracuda Ethel on the case to keep Grandma inside. She stayed with Grandma and made sure that she followed all of the doctor's orders. Mrs. Ethel made grandma lunch, gave her the medicine for her heart that we picked up from the CVS pharmacy on the way home from the hospital, and sat with her to keep her company. Mrs. Blanks promised to drop in on her as well. Grandma didn't like any of it, but she was out numbered. Mrs. Ethel, Antoine, Mrs. Blanks, and I were a united front.

We told the grandmothers that we were going on our weekly date and that we would return the next evening. We kissed them both and headed out the door with them both saying, "Have fun!" Grandma even said, "I won't be mad if you two make a baby." That was a surprise.

Before we could get out of the front door, Mrs. Ethel came down to whisper, "Are you going to find your Great-aunt Agatha?" I could not lie. I had to tell Mrs. Ethel where we were going. "Yes, Mrs. Ethel, we are going to find Agatha. Please pray that she will talk to me. I need some answers in order to move on in my marriage… in my career, my health, and in my life in general." She looked very worried. I understood her angst, but more important to me was the possibility of finding grace in my own life.

Antoine and I used the three-and-a-half-hour ride to have a self-directed mini counseling session. "So, how do you think we have been doing since we have been living apart?" he began. Honestly, I have truly missed him. I have missed living in my own house with my own stuff and my own rules; however, I could not deny the fact that the time apart has given me the opportunity to really get to know my grandmother and her history. My history.

I said, "It has had its highs and lows." High-Low is an exercise that we learned from our marriage counselor. At the end of each day, one of us could initiate the exercise by simply asking the other one, "High? Low?" Then as honestly as we can, we must tell the other, without details, the best part about our day and the worst part about our day. We are not to try to fix or help each other with the low, but only listen.

"High – getting Grandma home and settled comfortably. And also, having you make this trip with me. It is not anything that I would want to do alone or with one of my girlfriends," I said. After thinking for a few seconds, I said, "Low – walking into the unknown."

My husband nodded. He could have probably guessed this would be my high-low without my telling him. He knows me so well. Our problems had nothing to do with our soul connection. "Your turn, Honey Bun," I quickly turned the exercise around to him. "High? Low?" I asked. I could not wait to hear what he had to say.

"High- spending time with you outside of the counselor's office. Low- ..." he said, He thought for several seconds. The car was completely quiet. I waited impatiently. I wanted to yell, "Say something!" All I know is that he better not say that he had been getting high or going to the strip club.

Finally, he said, "I honestly do not have any lows. I'm clean. I'm with you. Mrs. Toni is doing better. She and Mrs. Ethel are acting like they like me and like I am really a member of this family. Even my mother has come out of her decades-long depression shell and left the house a few times. Babe, I'm good. For the first time in a long while, I'm high on life. I love you. I want you to come home. I'm ready to start a family." He grabbed my hand. I could feel all of the passion that his words conveyed, but I had to be sure.

"Antoine, are you sure that there is nothing else that you want to tell me? Is there anything else that I need to know?" I asked softly.

Antoine shocked me by admitting, "I have been calling the 1-900 sex lines since you have been gone Karen. I know you are going to say that is still wrong, but the counselor said it's a step down from pornographic movies and strip clubs. We are working on getting me completely healed and off of the phone sex. Okay? Please don't be mad. Work with me Baby Cakes. I swear I will let that go too."

All I could do is sit there and stare at the road. The all too familiar pain that was ever-present in my stomach now, suddenly worsened. He tried to get me to respond, "Say something Karen," he pleaded. I let go of his hand to rub my temples. I requested, "Let me have a moment, Antoine. I need to process this."

Antoine had been keeping me abreast of his private counseling sessions. Or so I thought. He never mentioned the sex lines. He never mentioned still working on a particular part of his sex addiction. I was a bit disappointed. People were lying to me left and right. There were keeping important information from me and I was sick of it. I am always my true and authentic self with everyone, but especially with my love ones. Why couldn't they show some reciprocity? I know…I won't tell them that my stomach pains are getting worse and that I have a doctor's appointment next week. I believe that there may be a serious problem, maybe cancer, but I'll keep it secret.

I finally said, "Okay Antoine. You have promised to stop calling the 1-900 numbers for phone sex. I believe you, but I will not move back home yet. I still need a little more time. Let's not discuss it any more on this trip. Let's just wait and discuss it in our counseling session with Dr. Smyth." He was happy to put it on the back burner for now.

Chapter 21

Oh Lord, maybe I should not have come.

We arrived in Chicago around 5 p.m. We decided to check into the hotel, then have dinner someplace nice. Seeing as how it was the dinner hour, I didn't want to disrupt Aunt Agatha and her family at their table. I'm pretty sure that she has a family because several people with the same last name all have the same address. I hope it's her.

Dinner was delicious. We had fresh sea food and succulent dessert. The conversation was light and fun. We laughed about old times, especially about things from our childhood. Back then, Antoine lived close by, but not close enough to come over by himself at his age. Since his parents did not keep a good eye on him, he was over every day anyway. After a few hours of playing ninja warrior, taking turns riding on my bike, and drinking water out of the garden hose, we would hear his mother call out from afar, "Antoine Jamar Blanks!" He would zoom home.

After paying the check, Antoine took one of my hands in both of his. He raised it to his mouth to kiss it, and before he could, I got hot all over. He planted his kiss in the palm of my hand. I had to immediately snatch it away in order to assuage away the internal flames I felt that were about to make me combust with desire for him. He knew he had me.

"Let's visit Great Aunt Agatha tomorrow Baby. We can go back to the hotel and order a bottle of champagne. I am a little tired from all that driving. You look like you could use some rest too," he tried to convince me. I was tired, and my stomach was still a little queasy, but there was no way that I was not going to the house I believed was where all my answers were.

"No way! We are going to that address right now. And if that is not the right one, then we need to go to the other address a few miles away. One way or the other, someone is going to tell me if Grandma is a monster or a mother just protecting her child's child. I need to know if my mother felt pressured into not coming back for me, or if *she* is the true monster," I explained.

At first, we drove in silence. This time it was comfortable silence, not like earlier. I almost fell asleep. Antoine interrupted my blissful descent into unconsciousness, what Grandma and I used to call Sleepy Land when I was a child. "You know, Karen, people don't understand what it is like for something as wicked as addiction to have a hold of you and won't let go. It is not a choice, no more than having diabetes and epilepsy. Sure, your first time using, you may have had a choice. But if that addiction gets its claws in you when you are just a kid, when you don't really know any better. When you don't know enough or have enough foresight to know what the possible outcomes could be…" he said, but his voice trailed off.

"I can understand how it overtook your mother. She was hurt. She was hurting so badly that she would rather be dead. She did not take her life probably because of you, Karen. So instead, she killed herself on the inside. She wanted to feel numb; not feel anything inside after losing her husband. That way, she thought that she could still be a parent to you. Or maybe she didn't think about it at all. All I am saying is once it got in her system, I mean like really took ahold of her, she didn't have a choice in the matter. Then, Mrs. Toni, someone she knew loved you as much as she did herself, came by that last time and basically gave her an ultimatum. The drug chose for her," he finished explaining.

We pulled up in front of the beautiful, magnificent home. The grounds were immaculately manicured. I grew up in a modestly nice home, but this was a newly built dream home. Antoine and I looked at one another. Neither of us knew what to say. We got out of the car. Antoine came around to my side of the SUV and took my hand. He said, "Okay Babe. Here we go." I was so nervous. My heart was pounding so hard, I could hear it in my ears. I also had butterflies, but not the usually pains I feel during stressful situations.

We walked up the long walkway, passed the semi-circle driveway where three nice cars were parked, and stood in front of the glass door. I took a deep breath and rang the doorbell. Antoine was rubbing my back. I wanted him to stop it and keep rubbing at the same time. Oh Lord, maybe I should not have come.

A man came to the door. He was already talking to someone inside, so he was looking over his shoulder. When he finally turned to say hello to us, his breath caught in his throat. "Oh, hi. How can I help you?" he finally said. He was about thirty years old. His hair was just staring ton turn grey around the temples. He was dressed in jeans and a plain blue t-shirt. He kept blinking his eyes. He wasn't smiling, but it was hard to read the expression on his face.

"Hello. Is Agatha Tanly-Reed available?" I asked. After blinking a few more times, the man suddenly wiped the confused look from his face and inquired, "Who's asking?"

"My name is Karen..." and as I was saying my last name, the man said it with me. "Edmonds-Blanks," we both uttered in unison. Then my mouth fell open. Who is this man? How did he know my name? There could only be one answer. This is where Agatha lives.

The man opened the door wider and motioned for us to come inside. "Please, come in," he said. Antoine and I walked in. I introduced my husband to this stranger. "This is my husband, Antoine Blanks. We drove all the way from St. Louis…" Again, the man interrupted because he already knew what I was trying to tell him. "Yeah, I know where you all are from. Come on in and have a seat. I'll get Gr…Agatha for you," he said. He escorted us to a room with a sectional couch, plush chairs, and a fireplace. Before he turned to leave, he said, "I'm Anthony. My friends all call me Tony."

When the man left the room, Antoine and I started talking to one another at the same time. He was saying, "Oh my God! I cannot believe that we found her on the first try. This is incredible!" and I was saying, "It's her! It's really Agatha. We found her. And this man has the same name as my grandmother!" Then we both responded to the other, but still at the same time, "I know, right!"

The man came back into the room. He sat down on one of the chairs directly across from the part of the couch that Antoine and I were sitting on. He clasped his hands together and declare, *Agatha*," putting a strange emphasis on her name, "will be right down. I'm her grandson. I bet you are wondering how I know who you are, right?" I don't know if it was nerves or if Antoine and I should have rehearsed what we would say, but we began talking at the same time again. "Yes, we are," we sang. I looked at him and he chuckled. "Go ahead, Babe. I'm sorry," Antoine acquiesced.

"It's okay, man. I get it. You have to protect your woman. I'm a stranger, so I get why you are taking the lead. I don't know if Karen here likes it so much," then he looked at me and added, "You are just like your grandmother," then he laughed and clapped his hands softly. At that moment, we heard footsteps coming toward the living room. A very small woman using a cane appeared in the doorway. "Tony, come over her and give me a hand, please," she said. Even her voice sounded just like my grandmother.

We all stood up at the same time. This woman's very presence commanded respect. She was beautiful. With a full face of makeup, diamond-pearl earrings and necklace, and an elegant hairstyle, she floated into the room. It didn't seem that she needed the cane. Tony lightly took her by the elbow and led her toward us. She stood in front of me and smiled her Grandma-Toni smile at me. And her Grandma-Toni eyes sparkled as she did so. I immediately felt right at home. I wanted to hug her, but instead, I extended my hand to shake hers and said, "Hello Auntie Agatha. I'm Karen Edmonds Blanks, your great-niece.

Agatha took me in her arms. She hugged me like she had known me all of my life. She stepped back, looked at me and then hugged me again. Finally, Tony cleared his throat then said, "Karen, this is *Agatha* Reed. Gracie, let the girl breath." We all laughed. Antoine and I exchanged perplexed looks. Not understanding why Tony called Aunt Agatha Gracie, I just said, "It's okay. I can breathe later." There was more laughter. Agatha finally spoke, "I am so happy to officially meet you, Karen. Please, everyone, have a seat." I wondered what she meant by *officially*.

Tony led Agatha to a seat. We all sat down. I could hardly wait to get through all of the pleasantries and talk about the past. "I trust you all had a nice trip, so tell me, Karen; how did you find me and how can I help you?" Agatha said as if she was reading my mind. Antoine said that we did have a good trip. He started telling her about the sea food restaurant we went to. Politely, Agatha said, "That's very nice, dear," then turned her attention squarely toward me. She just looked at me and waited. I was speechless.

Suddenly, I could not talk. A tear rolled down my cheek. Antoine took my hand and announced, "She is just happy to have found you, ma'am." Tony told Agatha that Antoine was my husband. "I know," she said. "I know everything about my sister and her granddaughter."

See, that is what I mean. I want to know *how* she knows about me, but the words would not come out. So, Agatha said, "Why don't I just start at the beginning and tell you everything that I know. Stop my any time you have a question. How does that sound dear?" Aunt Agatha said tenderly. I nodded. "Well, Toni and I are half-sisters. Toni and Agatha are not our real names," she said matter-of-factly. "My name is Grace, Sweetheart. And your grandmother's real name is Agnus." Well damn!

It looks like I have finally found the grace I have needed in my life.

Chapter 22

I felt broken deep down in my soul.

Aunt Grace noticed my shock, but she kept going with her tale. What she laid out before us was quite an incredible tale. It did, however, mimic my grandmother's story in several ways. Grace continued,

> *Our mother was a bit older than our father. They had three children and apparently Papa grew tired of having an older woman. He left their home and mother didn't know if he would ever come back. The man across the road nearby had just lost his wife to cancer a few years before. He would come over and help mama with different things around the house. He even gave her food for her children. A few months later, mother was pregnant with this man's child, but daddy came back. The man was hurt but respectfully stayed away. When Papa realized mother was with child, he was not angry with her. He was angry with himself for leaving her all alone and allowing such a thing to happen to her. When your grandmother was born, they named her Agnes. The next year, Mother and Papa were pregnant with me. When I was born, they named me Grace.*
>
> *When we were about two and four years old, we were playing outside in the yard around the large tree like we did every day. Usually Papa would come walking up the road and when us kids saw him, he would run toward us and we would run toward him. But on this day, he pulled up in a car and a woman got out. She told us to get in the car because Papa wanted to take us for a ride in his new car. Papa beckoned for us, so we were very excited to get in the car. We did more than go for a ride, however.*
>
> *We drove for a very long time. It was supper time, so I got cranky and started crying. I believe my sister was scared and wanted to cry, but she was always very quiet. Finally, Papa pull the car over and the four of us got out. It seems to me that he was hiding the car behind a barn. I think I heard him and the woman say that they stole it. Anyway, dark was beginning to fall, and my sister and I were very hungry. The more we cried, the more the woman yelled at us. Papa didn't say a word.*

Eventually, we hopped onto a cargo train, and we all quickly fell asleep. When we woke up, we were in a strange town with strange people fussing over us, pinching our cheeks, and telling the woman, 'Oh Hellen, you sure have some beautiful children!' Still, Papa said nothing. We went to the house that was to become our home.

Popa and the woman re-named us Toni and Agatha. They even changed Toni's age and made her two years older. The woman taught us how to clean her house. She made us scrub it down every day. She beat us whenever we did it wrong and she rarely gave us anything to eat until Papa came home.

Papa stayed out all day and half the night. He was always drunk when he came home, and he would argue with the woman. Sometimes, they would even fight. We heard her say, 'How in the world are you going to leave me here with these kids all day and the oldest one isn't even yours?' Then he would say, 'One of these days I'm just going to keep right on walking past your front door and never come home again!' Then one day he did just that. He stopped coming home.

Well, as time went on one M'dere put Toni in school. Then, she and I would spend the day together. She let me drink her beer. She let me stay home by myself while she visited men. And when she came home with money, we would go to the store and buy food. Food that she made me cook, but when Toni would walk through the door from school, M'dere acted as if she had been doing the cooking all day. I never said anything. I never did anything. That is, until she threw hot soup on Toni one day. I was furious. I wanted to kill her. How could she hurt my sweet sister like that?

> *I hated M'dere. She constantly did evil things to us. She would lock us both in the closet, backhand smack Toni and burn her with cigarettes, and let her boyfriends come to our house and touch or kiss me while my sister was at school. M'dere always seemed like she was mad at Toni. When her boyfriend made advances on Toni, that made M'dere even madder.*

> *She wouldn't give us anything to eat for days after catching her boyfriend paying us more attention than he paid her. One time she started beating on Toni because she thought her boyfriend was flirting with her. As she drew her hand up to smack Toni down, the man came up behind her and grabbed her arm. The two of them started fighting and rolling around on the floor. They broke a lamp and the coffee table. M'dere finally got up and ran to her room. She came back with her pistol and fired a shot at the man. He ran out the door yelling, 'I'm going to tell the police you stole some woman's kids from Perth County!'*

Grace paused and asked me if I was okay so far and if I had any questions. I was okay. I also had many questions, but I did not know how to put them into words yes. I nodded and told her to please continue.

> *Well, after several more years of physical and mental abuse and after watching this woman torment the only person in my life I truly cared about, I left. What I mean is at first my mind left. I didn't think about any of the things I did. My spirit left too. I felt broken deep down in my soul. I knew what M'dere was doing was horribly wrong, but I just didn't think that I could stop her. So, I submitted to it all. But then I notice that was hurting my sister even more. I remember laughing at some of the stuff M'dere did to Toni, but it was just a way to keep her and the beatings off of me.*

> *Finally, I met a boy who truly seemed to care about me. He hugged and kissed me all the time. He bought me things and gave me whatever I asked for. He even helped M'dere out by bringing her things and giving her money for bills and such.*

Soon I found myself pregnant, but I did not want to bring a child into the horrid mess that I lived in. I told my boyfriend that I did not want to keep the baby. He took me to a woman's house who had a full-service abortion clinic in her backroom. I ended my pregnancy. Then I really felt very empty on the inside. I couldn't stand being in that house with that woman any longer, so I moved away. I didn't tell a soul not even my sister. I was afraid that if she asked me not to go that I wouldn't.

Once settled in our new place, I felt a little better, but not good enough to continue a physical relationship with my boyfriend. He was spending a lot of time running numbers, selling drugs, and hanging out with his friends smoking and drinking. He claimed it was the only way to take care of me. Actually, it was the only way for him to find intimacy in other women's beds. I believe that since I was not giving him what he wanted anymore, I was of no use to him, so he stayed out. I started hearing rumors about other girls he was involved with, but he always told me he loved me and there were no others.

Eventually, I grew tired of the lies and the lifestyle I lived with him. I knew it was just a matter of time before he would be caught, so again I ran. I packed a small bag, grabbed some money from his stash, and boarded a Greyhound bus to Chicago. The bus let me out at a station near a hotel. I paid for a room for a week and went job hunting every day. By day four, I had found a job in a department store selling makeup. I was so good at it that I moved up the ranks to finally becoming assistant manager. I threw myself into my work. I took other people's shifts when they were sick. I worked overtime. I worded double shifts during the holidays. All I did was worked. You look like you are starting to relax Karen. Any questions for me yet?

I did feel a bit more comfortable. I even found my voice. "So far, so good. You are telling me everything that I needed to know. I can tell that you and Grandma are a lot alike," I said. She fired back, "Yes, we are. We are fighters, Karen. And so are you." Then she continued,

> *Anyway, I found a small apartment owned by a very handsome man who thought the world of me. I was afraid to get involved with him, but he said he needed my help. He said he trusted me. You see, he owned several other apartment complexes and houses, but wanted me to manage the building I lived in. I figured it was a way to make some extra money, so I did. I also saved all of my money so that I could go to college.*
>
> *Soon we so fell in love. Oh Karen, we had such a grand wedding! And many years later we had two great children- a son, Christopher, and a daughter Elizabeth. As my children started to grow, I missed my sister very much. I went back to St. Louis and found out that Toni had left M'dere's house after they got into a big fight. I also learned that she got married to a really good man and had a son of her own. Toni became a nurse and worked hard too. She sounded a lot like me. The only difference is her child was taken from her in a terrible car crash and she was left raising her grandchild all alone. I felt so terrible about all of this, but I lost the nerve to face her. Karen, when I found Toni and went to her house, no one answered, but the woman next door came out and we talked. It was our old friend from the neighborhood,*
>
> *By now you know that I am talking about Ethel. She has kept me abreast of Toni's life and your life as well. She has sent me pictures of you both and clipping from the magazine you write for. She has told me everything about you and your grandmother, my sister Toni- I don't know why she kept that name. Ethel has even tried to encourage me and to come back and sit down to face Toni again. Ethel said sisters should talk, but I couldn't. I couldn't believe that Toni would want to have anything to do with me after I left her in that hell hole with Satan.*

My life turned out so wonderfully. I have seven grandchildren. Christopher has three sons and a daughter. Elizabeth has two daughters and a son. Both of my children attended college, graduated with honors, got married, and gave me those seven more blessings. My life is so full! I eventually went to college and earned a chemistry degree. I started my own line of makeup that was hugely successful. After several years, I sold the company to a major skin care company and made millions of dollars. My husband remained highly successful in real estate until he died just recently.

I suffered a very mild stroke and have had a little heart trouble since losing him, but my grandson, Anthony...Tony, and his family have moved in with me to help take care of me. I got this bigger house or all of us. It has been a great life, but then again so has yours. I've kept up with you every step of the way. I even knew that you were coming here to find me today. Ethel called me. She also said Toni was sleeping and that she was recovering from an issue with her heart. See, we are just alike.

Ethel said you were having some problems in your marriage and that you found out that your grandmother has been keeping an important secret from you. I imagine that you are upset by all of that.

Karen, I want you to hear me and hear me well. Your grandmother loves you more than anything else in the world, even though she never thought that her heart could love anyone after all of the pain and suffering she endured. She would give you anything in the world and she would do anything in the world for you. The very thought of anyone or anything harming even a hair on your head would make her go to the ends of the earth protecting you from it. If there is any doubt in your mind that you are Toni's sun that rises and sets each day in her life, then put it to rest right here and right now! If I can know that from 350 miles away, then surely you know that with her right there in your heart.

Aunt Grace pointed to my heart. She was right. Grandma and I are a part of each other. She is my father's mother and has always done right by me. I love her, and I could not wait to get back home to tell her. It was time that I was the giver of grace.

Chapter 23

One year later

One year later, I found myself in a place that I had not been since I was a child. I was peacefully, wonderfully, joyfully happy. I left Aunt Grace's house last year after a hearty late night meal and relinquishing to her pleas to spend the night at her house. My cousin Tony gave Antoine a tour of the house. They never made it back from the billiards room, which was fine because Aunt Grace and I continued to talk more over coffee and cake. She made her sweets from scratch just like Grandma and Mrs. Ethel.

I called home to check on my two grandmothers – Thing 1 and Thing 2- the most mischievous people that I know. Mrs. Ethel said that Grandma was sitting in a chair by the window looking out at her garden. She ordered Mrs. Ethel to get the neighbor's son to come over and pull up the weeds from around all the precious items she intended to feed her family with.

I was finally able to communicate my thoughts and questions about the events that Aunt Grace told me. She really didn't say anything very different than what my grandmother had told me. She just helped me to put on my grace glasses and see that what my grandmother did was what she thought was best for me. She loves me and was only trying to save me from a bad situation. This is a lesson I needed to apply to my marriage and life in general.

One of my questions was, "So, Grandma never knew that Mrs. Ethel was keeping in touch with you and telling you everything about our lives?" Aunt Grace quickly said, "Oh no, my dear! I made Ethel promise to never tell Toni that she and I talked on the phone every week. She sent me pictures from your first day of kindergarten, high school and college graduations, your wedding, and so on." Wow, Mrs. Ethel is a Fort Knox secret keeper. I am going to have to sit down with her and get the full story about her past life too. Sounds like it could be the basis for my first book.

When we returned from Chicago, I moved back home with Antoine a few months later. Things have been running very smoothly. Of course, he still shops a lot and is always bringing home new clothes and shoes. And I am cooking and baking up a storm. He says that I am trying to make him fat so that no one else will want him. "Don't worry Baby Cakes, I don't want anyone else but you anyway," he is always saying. That may be true, but I cannot afford to get fat yet, so Bria and I work out in the gym after work three days a week. She stopped doing my hair because she says all I do is sweat it out anyway. She is right; I work hard in the gym.

Antoine has not used any drugs nor watched any porn. He stopped calling the sex phone line once we returned from our Chicago trip. He said that he really enjoyed our time together. He also said that he never wanted to do anything that would jeopardize the relationship again. He goes to therapy meetings for sex addicts three days a week; the say three days that I am at the gym. We each have a lot to talk about when we get home. At night, we cuddle together and talk all about the progress we are each making.

I decided to tell the family about my stomach pains. They were aware that I was having them but had no idea they had gotten as bad as they were. Antoine and Grandma went to the doctor with me. The doctor said it looks like I may have ulcers. She ran many more tests, however. I really wanted to get to the bottom of the issue and fix it because I was really ready to have a baby.

Grandma and even Mrs. Ethel have had one thing, or another happen to their health this past year. It has never been anything serious, but it has taught me to treasure them more. I finally got them to agree to live together under one roof. I promised them that once I got pregnant, that Antoine and I would move in whichever house they did not live in. That way, we would all be neighbors. Now, let's just see which house they would choose.

The best part about the year is that Grandma and Aunt Grace have been talking. We all went to Chicago for Aunt Grace's birthday. Tony and his wife, Tiffany, planned the party. Aunt Grace knew about the plans, but what she didn't know is that she would come face to face with a sister she had not seen in over fifty years. They spoke on the phone pretty regularly once we got back from our Chicago visit and agreed that they would "get together soon," but Aunt Grace had no idea that soon was now. Grandma and the rest of us would be at the festivities. Once she saw her sister, she cried, "You are the best gift I could ever receive!"

Aunt Grace and her son and daughter came to St. Louis for Grandma's birthday a few months later. We could not fool Grandma; she knew that her sister, niece, nephew, and seven great-nieces and nephews were coming. What she did not know is that Tony, whom Aunt Grace named after her own sister, had had a grandchild a few weeks prior. He had asked his son and daughter in-law to please name the baby after his Aunt Toni and they did. Grandma didn't know that the baby had been born and her parents were bringing her to the party as well. Little Bella Antonia was placed in her Great Aunt Toni's arms during the party. Grandma looked down at the baby with tears in her eyes. Bella looked up at Grandma a cooed. Grandma said, "Now, this is what real grace feels like."

GRACE –

free and unmerited favor

Thank you

Many thanks to everyone who has been encouraging me to finish and publish my book. And BIG THANKS to everyone who supported me and purchased it.

Special Thanks to Jill Mittendorf at Graphic Connections Group for lighting a fire under me and holding me accountable for getting my finished product to your printing press. I would still be "writing a book" if you had not insisted that it was time for me to be an author. Thank you!

LaKesha, thank you SO, SO much for helping me to edit my work. And you didn't stop there. You sold the book for me at the book release party and you helped Si set up for it. You're the best!

Thanks, Brother-in-law for the love, support, and the bomb Foreword! I know I'm your favorite sister-in-law (I won't tell the little sister – wink, wink). B., I also want to thank you for being an example for me to follow and for inspiring me to do my thing. You helped me to see that I really could put out my books.

I would not be anything good that I am today, not even a writer, if it was not for my mother, Marcia Marie Kindall. Mom, you instilled a love for words in my heart. Rest in heaven, Mom! Xoxo

And what is a writer if she is not also a reader. Big thanks to my grandmother, an avid reader, who is also responsible for helping me fall in love with words. Nana, I know you are in heaven reading Reader's Digest and working crossword puzzles. Rest peacefully.

Speaking of love, I would be remiss if I didn't thank my babies, Damion and AJ. Sons, you all taught me what unconditional grace really is. I pray that I have been an example of pure love for you and that you see God in me. Be blessed men of valor.

From the bottom of my heart, to the depths of my soul, I thank my Creator for all things that are good. For everything good is God and He is everything good. Better is one day in Your courts than thousands elsewhere, Father God. In Jesus name, Amen!

Much love to you all!!!!!!!!!!!!!

Coming Soon…

Look for my new book on the subject of mercy, where one of the characters will be loosely based on my *maternal* grandmother and her side of the family! It will be epic!

Follow me on social media

Facebook@acesreadforlife
Twitter@HouseAces
LinkedIn@Aces Literary-House
Instgram@adriennesmith

Feel free to email me anytime

acesliteraryhouse@yahoo.com

About the Author

Adrienne C. Smith was nicknamed Angel the day she was born. If you ask most people who know her, they would say she lives up to that name. She was born in St. Louis, Missouri and has traveled to a few other parts of the world. On her travels, she has met lots of people and made lots of friends. She loves listening to their stories – the good, the bad, and everything in between.

With a master's degree in Media Communications and a M.Ed. in Secondary Education/Reading Literacy, she decided to embark on a career in which she could turn some of the stories she has heard into must- read books. She works as an Adjunct Professor and owns her own company, ACES Literary House, and loves sharing stories with all of her students as well.

Adrienne loves to read and write. She also loves spending time with family and friends, taking pictures, scrapbooking, listening to music (especially live music), and watching old movies. She hopes to one day attend the Cannes Film Festival; and to one day see Elton John and Alicia Keys in concert.

Adrienne has two sons: one by birth and one bonus son. She also has one godson, one nephew, four nieces, and a niece in heaven whom she is sure is watching over her just like her parents and grandmother are. And as you may have guessed, she shares cool stories that them all.

Adrienne wants her readers to enjoy some of the stories that she "spiced up and mixed around" into her fictional tale. She says, "This book has been on a low simmer for over twenty years, so to finally share it is a dream come true!"

Made in the USA
Columbia, SC
29 January 2019